Rosebud
and Other Stories

INTERSECTIONS

ASIAN AND PACIFIC AMERICAN
TRANSCULTURAL STUDIES

Russell C. Leong
GENERAL EDITOR

Rosebud
and Other Stories

Wakako Yamauchi

Edited by
Lillian Howan

University of Hawai'i Press
Honolulu

In Association with
UCLA Asian American Studies Center
Los Angeles

Library of Congress Cataloging-in-Publication Data
Yamauchi, Wakako.
  Rosebud and other stories / Wakako Yamauchi ; edited by Lillian
Howan.
    p.   cm.—(Intersections)
    ISBN 978-0-8248-3260-5 (pbk. : alk. paper)
    1. Japanese American women—Fiction.   2. Japanese Ameri-
cans—Evacuation and relocation, 1942–1945—Fiction.   I. Howan,
Lillian.   II. Title.   III. Series: Intersections (Honolulu, Hawaii)
    PS3575.A447R67 2011
    813'.54—dc22
                                                2010026340

University of Hawaiʻi Press books are printed on acid-free
paper and meet the guidelines for permanence and durability
of the Council on Library Resources.

Designed by Wanda China
Printed by Sheridan Books, Inc.

Contents

Foreword

Wakako Yamauchi writes of the soul, the spirit hidden beneath the surface. Secret desires, unfulfilled longing and irrepressible humor flow through her stories, writings that depict the life of Nisei, second-generation Japanese Americans. Through the medium of her storytelling, the reader enters the world of desert farmers, factory workers, gamblers, housewives, con artists and dreamers, the bitter and the ever-hopeful.

Wakako Yamauchi was born in Westmorland, in the farmlands of the California Imperial Valley. Her birth certificate states her date of birth as October 25, 1924, but, as was common in farming communities, there was a delay in recording her birth, and she was actually born a few days earlier. She was named Wakako Nakamura, the third of five children. Her parents, Yasaku Nakamura and Hamako Machida, were Issei, immigrants from Shizuoka Prefecture in Japan.

Since the California Alien Land Law prohibited Asian immigrants from owning land, Yamauchi's parents were forced to move continually throughout her childhood, as the leases expired on the land they farmed. When Yamauchi was thirteen or fourteen years old, she began reading the English section of back issues of *Kashu Mainichi* during breaks from farm work—her father bought stacks of the newspaper to use as brush covers pro tecting the crops from frost. Yamauchi was fascinated by a regular column, signed anonymously as Napoleon Says. The column recounted daily life in a way that inspired Yamauchi. In one of a series of interviews at Yamauchi's home in Gardena, California, in 2007 and 2008, she told me that the writing "validated our lives—the food we ate, the fights we had with our siblings, the daily routine of the Japanese family." Yamauchi could not tell the identity of the mysterious Napoleon, but she was impressed that someone could transform the ordinary events of her life into compelling writing.

Following the disastrous failure of their lettuce crop and the Imperial Valley earthquake, Yamauchi's family left farming and moved to Oceanside, where they ran a boardinghouse for itinerant Japanese workers. Among the Japanese American community in Oceanside, Yamauchi learned the identity of the writer of Napoleon Says. Yamauchi confesses that she had been thinking, "Boy, I could go for this guy"—but instead she discovered that the author was Hisaye Yamamoto, a young Nisei woman only a few years older than she was.

In 1941, when Wakako Yamauchi was seventeen and a high school senior, war broke out between the United States and Japan. Yamauchi would not finish high school; instead she was interned along with 120,000 Japanese Americans incarcerated in ten concentration camps under Executive Order 9066. Yamauchi and her family were forced to leave their home in Oceanside for the Poston Relocation Center in the Arizona desert.

In Poston, Yamauchi began working as an artist for the camp newspaper, the *Poston Chronicle*. Hisaye Yamamoto, the enigmatic writer of Napoleon Says, was a staff writer, and it was during their work for the *Chronicle* that the two young women began their lifelong friendship.

Near the end of World War II, Yamauchi was released early from camp to work in a candy factory in Chicago. While in Chicago, she received word from her mother that her father was gravely ill. Yamauchi took the train back to Poston, only to discover upon arrival that her father had already died from bleeding ulcers. The internment camp was closing and Yamauchi, her mother, and her siblings were among the last group to leave—Yamauchi remembers her mother carrying her father's ashes in a container on her lap during the train ride out of Poston.

Yamauchi followed her family to San Diego and then attended night school at Otis Art Center in Los Angeles. She met her husband, Chester Yamauchi, and they were married in 1948. Their daughter Joy was born in 1955. During the postwar years of family life and raising her daughter, Yamauchi began writing fiction. She recalls that as she wrote, her fiction steadily moved "closer to what I knew—reaching in there and searching for the truth."

Henry Mori, editor of the bilingual Japanese-English newspaper the *Los Angeles Rafu Shimpo,* knew of Yamauchi's artistic work for the *Poston Chronicle* during the Internment, and, in 1959, Mori invited her to illustrate the holiday edition of the *Rafu Shimpo.* Yamauchi's husband Chester suggested that she negotiate a deal with Mori: she would illustrate if Mori would publish some of her stories. Mori agreed, and, beginning in 1960, Yamauchi published a story a year in the *Rafu Shimpo.*

In the early 1970s, Hisaye Yamamoto contacted Yamauchi to tell her that a group of young writers—Frank Chin, Jeffrey Paul Chan, Lawson Fusao Inada, and Shawn Wong—were organizing an anthology of Asian American writings. Yamamoto urged Yamauchi to submit her writings, and she sent several stories. Shawn Wong sent her an acceptance letter, writing that the anthology would publish Yamauchi's story "And the Soul Shall Dance." The anthology was the groundbreaking *Aiiieeeee!* (Howard University Press, 1974). In his authoritative introduction to Yamauchi's first collection of stories and plays, *Songs My Mother Taught Me* (Feminist Press, 1994), poet Garrett Hongo sets forth the pioneering importance of *Aiiieeeee!*

> The anthology introduced two generations of Asian American writers and inspired another generation to write as well, creating a renaissance of interest in writers, either out of print or writing in obscurity, who had reached maturity in the forties and fifties. These writers included Filipino Americans Carlos Bulosan and Bienvenidos Santos, Chinese Americans Louis Chu and Diana Chang, and Nisei writers John Okada, Hisaye Yamamoto, Toshio Mori and Wakako Yamauchi (a grouping that constituted, retrospectively, a kind of generational literary cohort).

Mako, the artistic director of East West Players, an Asian American theater in Los Angeles, read "And the Soul Shall Dance" in *Aiiieeeee!* and urged Yamauchi to write a play based on her short story. Mako told Yamauchi that it did not matter if the play was a hit or a miss—only that she keep the feeling that she had conveyed in her story. Mako's encouragement gave Yamauchi the confidence to begin writing her play, and she wrote six drafts before completing *And the Soul Shall Dance.* East West Players produced her play to packed houses in Los Angeles in 1977, and KCET in Los Angeles then produced Yamauchi's play for PBS, airing it nationally in 1977 and 1978.

Yamauchi would continue to write several critically acclaimed plays, among them *The Music Lessons, The Memento,* and *12-1-A.* Her plays were performed on stages from New York and New Haven to Los Angeles and Honolulu, garnering several prestigious awards. In 2001, Mako and Yoichi Aoki translated *And the Soul Shall Dance* into Japanese and produced the play in Japan. Invited to Tokyo and Kyoto for the performances of her play, Yamauchi reflected that her writing had come full circle—that the longing and unspoken courage of the Issei and their descendants had finally been allowed to return home.

Wakako Yamauchi wrote the stories collected in *Rosebud* when she was in her seventies and early eighties. Nothing fancy, she said—she wanted no artifice or embellishment, nothing superficial. She was concerned only with the clarity of her language and "telling the story, getting as close to the truth as I can." These stories, written in Yamauchi's later years, focus on conveying an interior truth that is deeply personal and often hidden from external perception. The historical constraints on Yamauchi's life—the Alien Land Law, segregation, the Internment and its aftermath—restricted the external freedom of much of her early life, yet through her writing Yamauchi transcends the limits imposed by the time and place into which she was born.

Yamauchi considered naming this collection *Taj Mahal,* after her play and the sublime monument built to love, for "we all need love," she explained as she discussed the collection's title: "Isn't that what life is about?" In the end, though, Yamauchi chose *Rosebud,* after the enigmatic word uttered by the dying protagonist of *Citizen Kane,* the classic movie based primarily on the figure of William Randolph Hearst, the powerful newspaper magnate. Hearst fanned hysteria against Japanese Americans through sensationalist journalism, paving the way for Executive Order 9066 and the Internment. In her story "Rosebud," Yamauchi recounts how Hearst "was building San Simeon, filling his castle with treasures of the world"— further illustrating the power Hearst wielded, the abuse of which effectively ended Yamauchi's formal education and stripped her and her family of their personal liberty and property. Yamauchi writes, though, that for all the power and wealth that he controlled, Hearst could not have the one thing he so desired, something that he had perhaps lost even before he knew of its importance—discovering too late that whatever Rosebud represented, it could not be controlled with power or "bought for all the gold in the world." With clarity and restraint, Yamauchi allows us, her readers, to feel the interior preciousness of the soul's longing. Bittersweet, elusive, and true, what the soul most cherishes is something that cannot be bought or manipulated. It can only be felt, and here in Yamauchi's writings, it is revealed through the light of her words.

Lillian Howan

Acknowledgments

I give my thanks to Lillian Howan for editing this collection of short stories and for all the tireless energy and love and faith she has extended toward bringing this publication to life. There is no way I can fully express my appreciation. To my friend Garrett Hongo, who has helped me in countless ways for countless years, I humbly say, "Thank you for *Songs My Mother Taught Me*" and for your love and patience. Garrett had fulfilled a dream I had not yet dreamed. I am grateful to Hisaye Yamamoto DeSoto for showing me that certain things can be accomplished even with my limitations. And thanks to Billy Clem, Ross Levine, Emma Gee, Russell Leong, and the UCLA Asian American Studies Center, to John Esaki, Akemi Kikumura-Yano, and the staff at the Japanese American National Museum, and to Paul Spickard.

To Joy and her family and to all my old friends, I say, "Thank you." I thank the comrades at McDonald's Figueroa for your friendship and the reality check. And thanks to all my family and my friends who have shared their stories with me.

Thank you to Neeti Madan at Sterling Lord Literistic, Inc. And I thank you, Masako Ikeda, of University of Hawai'i Press.

Rosebud

This is the story of Mutsuko Okada, daughter of a Japanese picture bride and a farmer. Probably sometime before the Asian Exclusion Act of 1924, Mr. Okada, tired of hacking it alone on the Southern California hard scrabble, found himself a marriage broker—an urban guy hustling extra bucks in a small room off a dry goods store. Mr. Okada snared his bride with a picture, probably not his own, literary correspondence (number five of a group of seven—ambitious but romantic), a savings account (required by the US Department of Immigration and rented by the marriage broker), and a few hundred dollars for the fare and trousseau, also borrowed.

No doubt the bride was astonished to find a groom quite unlike his photo, small, unapologetic, and relentlessly affable. The other lies came piece by piece over the years and probably reinforced her perception that the world will always be a place unworthy of trust and empty of joy.

At that time it was customary among us Nisei (Japanese Americans) to shorten and cutesify our Japanese names, and we took to calling Mutsuko "Muttsy." If we had called her "Mitzy," she probably would still be using that name, but we called her Muttsy partly because it didn't suit her and mostly because she didn't like it. Not that she complained. She certainly was no dog. She was vivacious and bright. Very smart. She was an only child and seemed to have everything she wanted. We thought she was spoiled rotten.

We played mean games with her. We asked, "Muttsy, do you have everything you want?"

"Almost," she answered cheerfully.

"Everything? Do you have a diamond ring?"

"I don't want a diamond ring."

"Do you have a ruby ring?"

"I don't want a ruby ring."

"Do you have a Shirley Temple doll?"

"I don't want a Shirley Temple doll."

We knew she lied. Everyone wanted a Shirley Temple doll. A Shirley Temple doll took you right up to the gates of the temple—right up to white middle America.

"You don't want a Shirley Temple doll?"

"Nope."

"Do you want a carrot?"

"I have carrots."

"Do you want a watermelon?"

"Watermelons are out of season." She always outlasted us and smiled while we scattered.

After school Muttsy's mother waited for her on the dirt road. When she heard us laughing, she would call Muttsy in and shoo us on. Her father was more accommodating.

Looking at her mother's hard jaw and her father's unabashed smile, we perceived that he was hen-pecked and didn't care or didn't know it. I think now he was a man of great stamina and inner strength.

It was a time of prejudice and racism, and few of us wanted to be identified as the "other," the "yellow peril." It was important to be as American as possible, white American with the in-your-face attitude of the twenties, the flashing Ipana smile, hair swirling in the wind (Muttsy's was naturally curly, another reason not to like her), and airy dresses made for croquet on summer evenings. Muttsy's mother sewed; no Sears or Mode O'Day for Muttsy. After all, an only child. That's what my mother said. "What? Sew dresses? You think I have nothing better to do? There's six of you!"

"But only two girls," I wailed. The middle two.

"They're the worst," my mother said. "Always whining, always wanting things." Attention, affection. Then she said, *"Hito wa hito,"* which literally means people are people but implicitly: "People are people, and you are you." Or "Other people have their stupid priorities." Well, I already knew that, but Muttsy's priorities were more fun. Or "Would you jump off a bridge just because someone else does?" My American teacher gave me that one. Muttsy wasn't jumping off a bridge or anything, but she was already distancing herself from us turnip patch kids.

I didn't really like Muttsy. She wasn't mean or snooty; there just wasn't common ground or an invitation to intimacy. With her, I always wished I'd cleaned my fingernails or pinched together the hole in my sock or kicked off the chunk of clay from my shoe.

Because of the Alien Land Law (Asians were by law denied the right to own land), farmers had to move as leases expired. I didn't see Muttsy for a few years. Then suddenly we were back together at another school. In the meantime she had been promoted and I demoted (I flunked math. My mother said it was all right; I was too immature for the class anyway), so we were now two classes apart. She still flashed her brilliant smile, and she had a new name: Marian.

In the thirties Marian Davies was a popular movie star. We didn't know it, but she was mistress to William Randolph Hearst, the newspaper tycoon, best known among the Japanese as the racist owner of the *Los Angeles Examiner.*

Hearst was building San Simeon, filling his castle with treasures of the world: statuary, tapestries, paintings, and much more, and indoor plumbing and central heating, I should guess. Languishing among the works of ancient and enduring artists and philosophers, I suppose one feels a sense of sublime and eternal life. Was it really true (as Orson Welles had said) that despite his power and immense wealth, he still did not have all he wanted and that in his heart of hearts he hankered for what was lost long ago or maybe never had, not bought for all the gold in the world, not retrievable for all his yearning? The man wanted everything.

And he got most of it, but in the end he grew old and died like the least of us, and Marian Davies also faded and died. So? I only know what I read in the papers.

There was also Maid Marian, Robin Hood's consort, a name that conjured thick yellow braids, blue eyes, and gauzy sleeves.

Aside from the shortened Japanese names, very few Nisei had American names. We picked them up after we endured the mutilation of our given names at the hands of, or more accurately on the tongues of, of all people, our American teachers: Tom for Tsutomu; George for Jioji; Sam for Isamu; those are three of my brothers (Goro stuck with Goro); Nancy for Natsuko; Mary for Mariko; Hannah for Hana. My little sister was actually named Florence and Hana, which means flower, and she moved between these two. I tried a few myself but none stuck. Who but Muttsy would adopt such a name as Marian and with such tenacity? No one ever called her Muttsy again.

There are Japanese names that almost pass for Irish: Omori, Osato, Ohara, Omura. A few people added apostrophes after their O's so that at least on paper they passed for white (uncommon now with today's ethnic awareness). Both my names are immutably Japanese.

My mother told me to wear my name like a flag. "Japanese are poets and scholars. They are the smartest scientists, most skillful surgeons, most creative artists. *Bushido* is the essence of morality, courage, and loyalty. Remember that," she said.

"Well then, why doesn't everybody know it?" I asked.

"Those that do, do. Those that don't, don't want to know. That's why they treat us like this."

"Well then, why do you stay here?"

"Don't think I'm here because I *want* to be," she said.

My mother said she was from a merchant family—tea packers in Shizuoka. Her father was married twice; the first time to a woman who bore him no sons, the second time to her own mother, who also gave him no sons. The first daughter of the first wife married a man who took the family name to carry on the line, but he embezzled and bankrupted the company. The name was mud by the time my mother was ready for marriage, so the pickings were slim; the only serious offer came from an immigrant to America who had returned for a bride. That was my father.

That's what my mother told me. When my father heard this story coming, he grunted (sometimes snorted) and went outside for a smoke. He also had great stamina that I suspected contributed to the ulcers that eventually felled him. My mother never told this story to the boys. She loved her boys.

Much later I learned of other stories: of Chinese building railroads and dying by the hundreds, dynamited in tunnels, tumbling off mountains, frozen until the spring thaw; of California vigilantes; of lynchings, picture brides, runaway brides, girls kidnapped for prostitution. A history of endurance.

Anyway, when we met again, Marian was in sixth grade and I in fourth, so we moved in different circles. Those two years we were at the same school, she was out of my life. Later the Okadas moved to a beach town just as we finally did. The Great Depression and the Alien Land Law drove us all over Southern California—two years here, two there.

When Japan attacked Pearl Harbor, all Japanese and Japanese Americans living on the West Coast were incarcerated in ten camps in the most desolate areas of the United States. For reasons still debated today, whether for national security, for our own safety, or for economic or political reasons, none were exempt. Like us, Marian and her family were sent to Poston, Arizona. She could not distance herself from this one. I was almost out of high school.

I didn't see Marian much during those four years of incarceration; she lived on one side of camp and I on another. I worked cutting stencils for the *Chronicle,* a weekly sheet. I hated typing, but I had to do something. I hated kitchen work even more, plus my mother told me to get off my duff and find a job.

To cut a stencil you first insert the stencil, a sheet with a layer of blue emulsion on it, into the typewriter with the ribbon removed. Then you type your story in columns. The type cuts the emulsion. Corrections are made with a dab of fluid that seals the error. Then the type is corrected over the dried fluid. The finished stencil is fastened around an inked mimeograph drum. The ink seeps through the cut type and makes the printed sheet as the drum is turned. I was not a natural. Today with copiers everywhere, mimeographing is a lost process. I was not a good typist.

I made friends with one of the reporters at the *Chronicle* who simply fell apart laughing each time I reached for the correction fluid, cursing, my face dripping with anxious sweat.

"What're you going to do when we start a daily sheet?" Ruth cried, holding her belly.

Work all night, I guessed. Who answers questions like that?

"We oughta get a real typist in here. Girl in my block's a crack steno. You oughta see all the certificates on her wall. Number one in the state of California. Typing, shorthand, you name it. All framed."

"Well, get her over here then," I fumed. At these wages the paper could afford a crack stenographer. The ceiling for steno work was sixteen dollars a month, for typists like me, twelve, the same as for janitors and dishwashers.

"Well, she can't work," Ruth said.

"What's the matter? Broken fingernail?"

"Naw, her mother won't let her."

"Then you'll have to put up with me."

"You said it." Still laughing, Ruth thumped my back, and the correction fluid sloshed all over the stencil. Had to do the whole sheet over. Boy.

One day Ruth said, "I think her mother's daffy."

"Who?" I asked.

"Your crack steno—her mother." She liked to say that. She liked to rile me.

"My mom's nuts too." It felt good to get that one out. "And probably yours too," I added.

"Well, does *your* mom follow you around on your dates?"

What dates? "Where do you go on dates around here?" I asked.

"Well, you know she's really pretty, and the guys used to flock around her, but her mom was always skulking around."

"Where can you skulk around here?" A crack steno and pretty too. And guys all over the place.

"Well, you know, always hanging around half a block away, going to the canteen, mingling at the talent shows, waiting by friends' barracks. Waits hours. Never gives up. I've seen her. She scares the guys off. Girls too. She won't let her get a job. Completely isolates her."

On another day Ruth said, "Boy you won't believe what she told me. Your crack steno."

I was thinking, "Oh, shut up," but I said, "Oh, yeah?"

"She said when she was a little girl, her mother used to give her examinations regularly. Physicals."

"So did my mom," I scoffed. She pulled my ears once a month, looking into them with a homemade Q-tip. I swear that's why they're so long now.

"Did your mother check your hymen?"

"Hymen" leaped from my fingertips directly onto the stencil. "I don't want to hear it," I said, reaching for the correction fluid. "She should have put a stop to it."

"She did, finally."

"So what's the problem then?"

"Don't you think it's a little odd?"

"Yep."

"You aren't a very sympathetic person, are you?" It wasn't a question; it was a statement. "She knows you, you know."

This gal was simply not going to let me work. "Who?" I asked.

"Marian Okada."

Oh, boy. I got a sudden migraine and had to leave, deadline or no.

I walked out, planning to pick up some aspirin at the canteen, but continued past it and headed east. I didn't know where Marian lived and was thinking, how dumb to look for her like this on a hot day. I had almost started home when I heard my name.

Marian was sitting outside her barrack in dazzling white voile. She flashed her smile. "Hi," she said.

Nothing seemed to have changed. Not the smile, not the relationship. But we were older, earth-shattering things had happened, we were captives in this strange place, two of millions caught in a global storm. Still, here we stood as though nothing had changed. It was surreal: I had walked to her block and she found me. People seemed to be floating by on waves of heat. I was drowning in a headache.

"How are you?" she asked.

"Got a terrible headache," I said as if she really wanted to know. I wished I had a comb. "How've you been?"

"Pretty good," she said and she looked it. She was cool and unflappable.

I was thinking, "Boy, that Ruth. I ought to whack her with this migraine. I said, "Hot enough for you? How about getting something cold at the canteen?"

"Okay," she said and hesitated only a millisecond. "But I don't have any money."

"I got enough for a couple of sodas," I said, "but don't you go ordering no champagne and caviar, ha-ha." That's the kind of stuff that passed for humor in camp.

Marian got to her feet, and I almost missed her quick glance at the barrack window. We were not halfway to the canteen when Marian suddenly stopped. "I can't go with you," she said.

Did I see the flutter of a gray housedress half a block away? Oh, sure, there are thousands in camp, I thought, and at least a hundred are Issei (first-generation) women in gray housedresses. But skulking? Naw.

"Why not?" I asked.

"I just remembered I was waiting for someone. I'm expecting company," Marian said.

By the time I said, "Oh, okay, some other time then," I was talking to myself. Marian had disappeared. I went on to the canteen and bought a bottle of aspirin and a popsicle to lay on my head. Since I was talking to myself anyway, I said, "Heck, it's not my problem. Heck, I can hardly take care of myself, so why am I worrying about someone else?"

So when Ruth started on the next chapter of the saga, I told her to lay off. I didn't want to hear. But, as I expected, she went right on. She said Marian was in the hospital. She was found in the barrack snipping her clothes into tiny pieces. All of them.

"What happened? Who found her?" The beautiful white voile.

"Her mother. She was just snipping away...pieces no bigger than a thimble...in the dark."

"And her mother took her to the hospital?" It was inconceivable: a Japanese admitting to an emotional breakdown in the family.

"She tried to stop her, but, well, Marian had the scissors, you know."

"Huh???"

It turned out Marian didn't actually attack her mother. Ruth meant that with the scissors, Marian had the upper hand. The block manager quietly took her to the hospital.

Mr. Okada was typically not there.

When I went to visit Marian, she acted as though she were there for an appendectomy. I took some magazines. She said, "Oh good. It'll give me something to do."

Well, Marian didn't have to look hard for something to do. She stayed in the hospital for a few days and Ruth's next story was, "She's working now, you know. For one of those high-muck-a-muck white guys at Administration."

"How'd that happen? What about her mother? Didn't she object?"

"Her doctor got her the job," Ruth said. So that made it okay, I guess.

I hated to admit it, but it was a relief. Whether Marian liked it or not, I felt a kind of responsibility for her: me younger, dumber, and a country clod. After Ruth told me about the family abuse, I remembered Marian coming to school, so little, so pretty, so cheerfully enduring our teasing. I felt sad, regretful. Not for long, though. I am remarkably self-absorbed, and that saves me a lot of anguish.

I left the *Chronicle* shortly thereafter. There wasn't any point in torturing myself over a twelve-dollar job when I could torture myself for the same money doing more challenging work. There was an opening at the dental clinic, and I got in as a dental assistant. It was easier than cutting stencils. It was quieter, no mobs of young people traipsing in and yakking their jaws off. Just a lot of old folk who had neglected their teeth for years. You can bet there were a lot of extractions. That's what bothered me the most: the sucking sound of teeth being pulled. But it beat doing bedpans as a nurse's aid, the other available job.

Eventually I bumped into Ruth. After all, the hospital was her beat. She said, "It's a good thing you left. You did us a favor, you know." I didn't want to know, but, as usual, she was going to tell me anyway. "We've got a great gal now. She gets the work done in half the time. We're thinking of doing a biweekly now."

I played dumb. "That much news, huh?"

"Hell, this gal's a crack typist."

"Like your crack steno?"

"Interesting you should mention her."

I bit. "Okay, how is she?"

Well, her mother's worst nightmare came true. She started something with her boss, him a married man and white too, and, well, they whisked her out of camp."

"Who? When? They can't do that. She needs clearance to get out."

"Clearance is easy when you're in Administration. She might be preggers."

"How do you know? It's just a rumor and you're spreading it. It's just a rumor."

"Could be," Ruth said. "Want to write her? I got her address."

"No, I don't want to write her." Marian, Marian.

I wrote one letter but it was no good. She was a woman, and I was still a girl.

Ruth often irritated me. "Often" is an understatement, but I liked her a lot. Even so, as the incarceration stretched into years, we drifted apart. That is, if we were ever close.

It was hard to keep in touch with friends. It was hard to keep in touch with family. George joined the Nisei Battalion and is buried in France. Goro went to Chicago; my father died in camp of bleeding ulcers. Tom and Sam relocated to Seabrook, New Jersey, and called my mother and Hana to join them. I was invited too but stayed in camp by myself, rattling around the barrack that we once all shared until the West Coast was again open to us.

My mother had a hard time dealing with the scattering of her family, dealing with growing old, but I couldn't ask her to come to Los Angeles and share my dismal apartment and my meager salary at the belt factory. "Nothing is the same," she wrote. "It's the war. Papa is gone, George is dead, everyone is spread all over. It's the war."

But I was young and resilient. I got into courtship games and finally fell in love, and then it was bills and babies. Well, actually only one. I didn't want to do it like my mother: too busy for attention and affection. But even with just the one, I didn't find time. Ask my daughter; ask my ex-husband. They'll tell you I was distant, moody, and often sat silently at the typewriter. Me who hated typewriters.

Anyway, Ruth never wrote. Marian once sent a Christmas card that I didn't acknowledge.

So the years hurtled by. In 1963 a friend showed me a clipping from a Japanese American newspaper. "Nisei Woman Marries Prominent Economist-Educator," it said. "Marian Okada married Dr. Robert P. Bingham in a private ceremony in San Francisco's exclusive blah-blah-blah. It is the first marriage for Ms. Okada, 40, and the third for Dr. Bingham, 62, internationally known economist. The bride wore blah-blah." Even in the grainy picture, Marian looked radiant. The groom? All right for sixty-two, I guess. Everyone was looking old to me then.

Out-marriages were rare among us Nisei, and marrying into fame was a celebration for all of us. My friend said, "She must be awful smart.

Gosh, I wouldn't even know how to talk to an economist." My marriage was going to pot. I wanted to say, "Idiot. You can say, 'Dinner's ready,' can't you?" But I said, "Me neither." I didn't mention that I once knew Marian.

After I put my divorce behind me (it took two years, just as the books say), I tried to work at writing—nothing really serious: short stories, essays, just to keep busy. My daughter had flown the coop, and there was actually nothing left but the writing. Also, America was slowly coming to acknowledge ethnic diversity. And at fifty-five it was now or die trying. I went to an Asian American writers conference in San Francisco to see what other Asian American writers were doing.

I found that while I was sleepwalking through the housewife years, young writers were hacking a path toward recognition by telling *our* stories: immigrants and railroads, persecution and valor, love and alienation. I felt renewed as I packed to go home.

The hotel door was open. Marian peeked in. "They *said* I'd find you here," she said.

I hadn't seen her since her mother died and camp was closing. She had returned for the funeral and also to take her father away. She was so busy we hardly talked. We were twenty then.

God, we'd grown old. Well, thirty-five years, you know. But she looked great in a spring floral and a hat that picked up the pale pinks of her dress. "How are you, Marian?" I asked.

"Pretty good," she said. She looked it. She invited me to a dinner party that night. "Just a few friends," she said.

"I can't, Marian. My plane leaves in a couple of hours," I said.

"Well, change the reservation."

"Lot of trouble."

"I'll do it for you," she said. The quintessential secretary. I didn't answer. "Well, I'll drive you to the airport then."

"I can take a cab," I said. "You have a dinner to prepare."

"The caterer would rather not have me around anyway," she said. Caterer? For a few friends? I was glad to be going home.

On the ride to the airport we were like people skirting around quicksand, afraid to be sucked in, yet lured by curiosity.

"Wasn't that a nice conference?" I asked. "Nice" is a word we Nisei often use.

"Marvelous," she said, expertly taking a curve. She must have driven the highway hundreds of times chauffeuring important guests to and from the airport. "It's the first time I've been around so many Asians."

"You mean since camp."

"Of course. Do you know I write now?" she said.

"Oh, really? I write too."

"I know," she said.

Did she read my stories? Did she like them? I didn't dare ask. She might say, "They're nice" or "Immigrant genre has its charm" or "I know all those stories but 'other people' may find them interesting." And I'd have to say, "Well, not yet, they don't" or "That's just the point: I'm trying to validate our lives." Too defensive, that one.

Instead, I asked, "How's Dr. Bingham?"

She didn't notice my formality. I guess she was used to it. "Oh, he's okay," she said. "He's getting old." Forgetful? Senile? Depressed? Incontinent? Impotent? Dependent? Whatever, she could handle it.

I played it light. "Aren't we all? Do you have children?"

"No." Then she really wasn't pregnant when she left camp. Or if she was, did she give the baby away? Abortions were illegal then. "Do you?" she asked.

"One. I'm a grandmother now." Some people don't like to hear about grandchildren. "Do you hear from Ruth?" I asked.

"I lost touch with her long ago," she said. "I've lost touch with all my Japanese friends."

Well, it was true: Ruth *was* a Japanese friend. Once her best. I was a Japanese friend too. She continued, "It's really good to see you again. I didn't realize how much I'd missed you." I think she meant us Japanese. "I have to get in touch again," she said. "People need roots. People need homes."

Hadn't they treated her well? That adorable Japanese girl? I know: they can sting you without saying the words, without opening their mouths. They look through you like you're invisible. It's such a habit they don't know they're doing it. They forget you're there and don't introduce you, and when you call attention to it, it's, "Oh, I'm sorry," and you're expected not to feel anything. Even shop girls find you invisible.

"Welcome home," I said. Then I said, "We're easy." I could have bitten my tongue. Who was I to say that? It wasn't *my* exclusive club. But she sort of asked for that one. Well, she didn't hear me anyway.

When we said good-bye, we exchanged air kisses and addresses and promised to keep in touch. We didn't.

However, a few years later I got a manuscript in the mail. It was from Marian. Just the manuscript, no cover letter. I'm sure she was busy. Anyway, no explanation was necessary.

It was the story of a seventeen-year-old girl in rural Japan who stayed home with a fever while her family went to the village for the Festival of the Dead. She was seduced by the handsome boy from the next farm (was there another motive for staying home?), and for a few days she gorged herself in a feast of love while her unsuspecting family enjoyed the festival in town. When she found herself pregnant, the young man denied complicity and absconded. Both families ostracized her (disregard for tradition and ritual exacts its price). In shame and anger, the girl strapped the baby to her back and set out to find her lover. The baby did not live long, and the lover could not be found. Obsessed, she continued her search. Finally, well into her thirties, the girl was advised to offer herself as a picture bride and to marry a farmer in America. But she did not leave her anger behind. She brought along her bitter dowry.

It all made sense: the towering rage, the need to control, the obsession, the ruined lives.

So where was the rest of it: the story of the bride fueled with anger who returned every day, every day to the village in Japan, to the Festival of the Dead, to the betrayal; the woman engulfed in a fury that sloshed into her marriage and frightened a simple, good-hearted (if deceitful) man into helpless impotence? And what about the daughter she tried to protect by cutting her off from all possible relationships while showcasing her in delectable tissue voile, in virgin white? What happens to the girl who fulfills her mother's dire prophecy? Where was all that? What a karma!

Oh, heck, it was just a story. As a writer myself, I should know how a story grows, swerves, takes a quick turn, and eventually bears no likeness to the mother seed.

I didn't know what to say to Marian. I thought I'd just play dumb. I wasn't really that close to her. So I said the usual: Great writing! Powerful story! It stayed with me for days. I wasn't lying.

She didn't write back. She was probably busy with faculty teas, fund-raisers, charity work, and things. Or maybe writing wasn't a big deal with her, just something she knocked out in a couple of days, off the top of her head. Not a true story. With me, it's always pushing, pulling, reaching, and digging, searching for truth as though there was a real one somewhere. She was so competent, always knew what to keep and what to throw away. She could take care of herself. She'd done all right so far, hadn't she?

It wasn't tea and crumpets and student affairs that kept her busy after all. One day I read in the *Times* obituaries that Dr. Bingham passed away *after a long illness.* Coffee and tea and finger foods served daily no doubt; faculty and postgraduates trekking in, brows furrowed in concern, offering help, asking advice, and, by the way, a clarification of this theory or that before, before the irrevocable silence. But, of course, she'd have a housekeeper—she once told me she was allergic to dust. She'd not be there on cleaning days. She'd have a nurse too. And she'd have friends. Many friends. The obituary said *quietly in his sleep.* A coma?

I sent a card and asked if there was anything I could do. She called about a year later. She was cheerful. Well, there'd been a lot to do: Bob's books, papers, the funeral, the will, the money. She gave most of it away. Well, you know, she was his third wife, and there were offspring from previous marriages (although they'd disappeared for a lot of years) and even grandchildren. "It's only money," she said. And years of devotion, doormatting, ass kissing, all that, well, hardly measurable in dollars and cents, or engraved in gold, all that disappeared with the last warm breath. Along with some friends.

"He really didn't have that much interest in people," she said. "Only trends, free trade, international markets, things like that. I didn't get into it much. Just the paperwork, the secretarial work. I saved him a lot of money."

I made a lame effort. "Economics is the glue that holds societies together." I didn't even know if I made any sense. It didn't interest me much either except when the mortgage was overdue or the price of a decent blouse tripled or when taxes went up and I stopped buying books and started using my library card.

"He wasn't what you call an endearing person," she said. "They deserted us when his work slowed down. They came back when they needed more, and I think that proved something to him. That made him happy," she said.

It was like I thought. "What will you do?" I asked.

"Don't worry," she laughed. "I'm not *destitute*. Besides, there's social security and Medicare, remember?" Yes, we'd grown *that* old. "I think I'll try writing again," she said. "I've made a lot of dinners for a lot of agents. Maybe it's time to cash in some chips." For sure we will not go gently.

"Good luck," I said. I know how forgetful people are about widows, orphans, divorcées, and the elderly.

But we weren't dead yet. At least Marian wasn't. Within a year she sent me a national woman's magazine with a short story written by M. O. Bingham. It was a hilarious tale of campus life: of students and faculty jousting for power in hallowed halls, of thinly disguised ambition and greed in the upper strata of academia. Enviable writing. You couldn't tell that M. O. Bingham did not come from the great white middle class, that she was once a little Japanese American from a dysfunctional family. I only knew it from her small yellow Post-It. "Well, what do you think?" she wrote. "I was encouraged by your early critique. Remember? Thanks, M."

There's no law that says she must be bound to grungy stories of immigrant life, of racism, of mass incarceration in these United States, of searching for identity, of love in mixed marriages, of... What's the difference? People are people. And she had not forgotten the half-truths, and she had kept them alive in her heart (or was this only a half-truth too?). I felt like a hypocrite. But what the heck? It worked for her, as they say.

I did it again. I told her how I had enjoyed the story, remarked again about the great writing, and I omitted the disappointment. Anyway, it wasn't even a whole thought. Just a small prickle, a feeling that flashed by. She had no obligation or responsibility to... But I've said that already.

Last year Marian wrote another story. This one about love among the ruins, a December-December story. It was a romp in a meadow, a reawakening of sexuality. There was a sense of a last hurrah.

I knew something was going on. Sure enough, she called to say she was in love and would be marrying again soon, that she again enjoyed the thrill, excitement, and, yeah, sex. A drink from a forgotten well. Water to renew life.

"Geez, Marian, how old are you anyway?" I asked.

"Seventy-one," she said.

"Are you taking hormones or something?" I asked. My God, I haven't felt like that in years except once in a rare while, through reading or sometimes movies, safely at a distance where I can get beyond the drying skin, graying hair, flabby arms, the logistics—prenuptial agreements, cooking and laundering again—and more important: fragile egos, bruised feelings, sparring for power (it's important to be right, you know, even at this age), and the waiting, waiting, for his return. "You'd give up your freedom?" I asked.

"Well, I don't intend to," she said.

"Why don't you just live together?"

"No, I don't want to do that," she said. "We're getting married at the country club here. You're invited, you know."

"Oh, Marian, I can't go."

"It's all right," she said.

I'm happy for her. Genuinely. Am I envious? You bet. I'd give a bundle to feel that old surge again, to trust someone again. She met him at a *soirée*. He's part of the publishing world, family money, Republican. That's pretty far from her roots. Far.

I'm feeling a loss. I'm thinking she can never come back. But to what? I was never a real friend. I was among those who teased and laughed and tested her bravado.

Actually I haven't been a true friend to very many. Oh, I've lowered the bridge (another watery metaphor) three or four times only to let in invaders dressed as friends. They were Nisei like me. Japanese Americans.

Well, we are Japanese who let her down, starting from her mother who imposed her fearsome agenda on Marian; a father who could not be a samurai for her; me, offering only glib words; Ruth, looking for a surrogate rescuer; my mother, pushing Marian off as "other people." So? Don't we have the right to make mistakes too? Why are we more unforgiving of our own?

I'm probably making too much of this whole thing. Like everyone else, Marian is only staking her place in this unfeeling world. And it's not as if I should spend my days and nights, days and nights trying to figure it out, trying to tie up loose ends. Who am I anyway? God? It's not like my own life is so ordered or perfect or that I don't have other things to think about. Let it go. Let it go.

Marian and I are like paper boats (again water) launched together, bumping off to sea. We have both bailed water separately, we've glided past one another, sometimes hearing music from the other deck, sometimes profound silence. If she should reach the sea before me, would she whisper, "Rosebud?" I'd probably say something like "Citizen Kane."

Dogs I Owe To

On South Halldale Avenue, we set out our trash and garbage on Tuesday afternoons for Wednesday pickups. I sit at the window that faces the street in my daughter's room, now long vacant, and watch the sun go down. A dark speckled dog crosses diagonally from the other side and sniffs the bags of trash. He doesn't mark his territory—he has none. He sniffs and gnaws quickly through the opaque plastic and draws out what looks like the ham bone I had thrown out earlier. His eyes dart around, streetwise, and he disappears around the corner.

He is homeless, I know. Who would love such a homely dog, or, loving him, who would let him roam the streets, hungry, taking garbage from trash bags? In a few years he will be in the winter of his life, the years leaping by in increments of seven. I want to rush to my refrigerator for something for him—something tasty and nourishing. Maybe I will heat it a little, make it room temperature. But I do not move. He is gone anyway, probably gnawing the bone under a hedge somewhere. I do not move.

When I was a girl, my father brought home a little black puppy. It was either my sister or my brother, both older than me, who named him Dickie. He was one of Mary's last litter—Mary who'd grown fat and sloppy after so many pregnancies. Mary belonged to the Nakamuras, a family with the same name as ours but not related, who operated a boardinghouse in town for transient laborers. The hotel was located next to the Buddhist church that we attended every Sunday, weather permitting, and where we got our weekly dose of religion and Japanese language lessons. Mary would waddle to the churchyard, her flaccid teats swinging, and let us pet her.

My father did not often give us living gifts. Most of my early memories are of my mother, of cold winter mornings on the desert farm, of blinding sunlight, of shadows cast by the moon reaching at me on the way to the outhouse, of my sister and brother tormenting me, and of the comfort of dogs.

The dog before Dickie was Terry, and I suppose my sister or brother named her too, because it was only later, when I started first grade, that I read about Jack and his dog Terry in my primer. Before that I didn't know any American or English names for dogs.

Terry looked like a collie. She had a regal nose and long orange-brown hair and a beautiful white collar. I loved her, but I was very young and didn't understand much about love or loyalty or empathy and such things. She loved us, I'm sure.

But dogs must connect with dogs as people must connect with people. Even on that isolated farm, nature had its way, and Terry gave us a litter: twelve little squirming black and white wormlike creatures. My father let us each choose one to keep (provided they were male) and disposed of the rest in some barbaric way. Barbaric, I know, because he did an awful thing soon after; with a pair of enormous shears, he cut off the tails of each of our puppies. My mother thought this was an American ritual; she'd seen many pictures of dogs with short tails. My father said none of his dogs will show fear by tucking their tails under. The message was clear: Feel if you must, but don't show it.

The puppies whimpered until their wounds healed; I could feel their pain in my own nether regions. And one by one they died. My mother said it wasn't from the surgery. She said animals die; people die; it's the law of nature. My father said nothing.

Terry died a horrible death. I don't know exactly what preceded the incident, if you can call death an incident. I only remember standing with her by the chicken coop, idly pulling burrs from her hair. My sister and brother were at school (I was still underage). Suddenly Terry broke away and ran toward the house. I saw that we were standing on an anthill, and I thought ants had stung her or that I'd pulled her hair too hard. She ran round and round the house, hair flying and wattles of spit streaming from her tongue. My mother screamed at me to come into the house.

I'm not sure what happened next; I think my father called for one of the young Mexican men who worked at the ranch, because he was in the house with my father's rifle, crouching at an open window and aiming as Terry passed the window again and again. He waited and aimed. He took Terry with one perfect shot.

As she lay dying, he crushed her beautiful head with the rifle butt. He dug a hole and buried her before my sister and brother returned from school.

My brother said Terry had a disease called scabies or rabies or something. He said it was lucky no one else caught it too. My sister said Terry probably missed her babies so badly she went crazy from it. What did she know about grief at that age? I didn't tell anyone about pulling Terry's hair or standing on an anthill.

After Terry and her babies, we didn't have pets for a long time. I think now, my father was pretty generous to allow us those three dogs. I think now, my mother probably told him it was three or none. We already drove her nuts with our constant bickering and hollering for equal everything: equal servings, equal toys, equal space. Equal love. But three more dogs in that wild country wasn't such a big deal. Just a little more food, a little more cursing to get them to do their business away from the house. They got their protein eating desert animals. That's how Terry picked up rabies. I found out much later that the puppies died of distemper.

There was a time when my mother left us to work in San Pedro at a tuna cannery. She was away six months (I counted them) and sent us lots of special things like coats, underwear, Christmas presents for our teachers, sanitary napkins for my sister (we couldn't imagine what they were for, maybe injuries), and money for the farm. I learned about loneliness then.

My mother returned to us one rainy January night. Mr. Nakamura picked her up at the Greyhound depot and drove fifteen miles over mucky country roads to bring her to us. No one told me she would come home that night. I was shocked to see her. I clasped her waist, buried my face in her warm tummy (I was that small), and wailed.

Mr. Nakamura said, well, if it was that painful for me, he'd just take my mother back home with him. He pretended to be angry. Everyone laughed. I'm sure we were all happy to have her back, especially my sister who at twelve had been doing all the cooking and washing (on a washboard), but I was the only one who actually cried.

It was sometime later in the mid-thirties when my father brought

Dickie to us. In the Southern California desert, we were then witnessing an exodus from the Dust Bowl; dismally pale children ate dabs of paste in our two-room schoolhouse; others more daring stole apples and cookies from our lunch pails. Hitler had not yet invaded Poland. I was ten. Dickie had already lost his tail at Mr. Nakamura's boardinghouse. He wagged the stubs of it expectantly, joyously, the pain and loss already forgotten. What new adventures awaited him at this desolate place?

The Great American Depression was winding down, but there was little money on the average farm. We recycled our clothes and ate off the land. Meat was not a staple at our house. We didn't keep animals on the farm because it wasn't practical. At that time in America, noncitizens weren't permitted to own land, and Japanese, by law, were denied citizenship. Again, by law, land leases to Asian immigrants were limited to three years, so every two or three years, Japanese farmers loaded houses and farm gear on trucks to move to yet another barren patch of land. We were nomads; there was no hunkering down with large animals. It was too hard to herd them from place to place. We even stopped keeping chickens.

It was also before the advent of dry or canned pet food—not that we could have bought Dickie any. He was happy to eat leftover rice drenched in soy sauce. In spring he gnawed on yellow crookneck squash. He didn't like eggplant or tomatoes. He had on occasion mutton or lamb discarded by shepherds who passed through. He woke up happy to be alive, jumping and bounding in the sharp morning air. I didn't allow him to touch me with his dusty paws, especially when I was dressed for school, so he pranced parallel to me, leaping and dancing, happy with even this tiny space in the grand scheme of things.

I always tried to give him some of my good food: a scrap of meat, a crust of bread, the tiniest piece of my candy bar. I'd throw these to him (I hated the gluey feel of his saliva), and he'd catch them midair, or, if he missed, he'd find them in the dust, even the smallest crumb. Sometimes the dirt clod was bigger than the treat, but he'd enjoy them both and look at me gratefully and expectantly. That look, that trust, went directly to my heart.

And when I was sad, he shared my grief. It was before television, and there was little to distract a kid from those vague feelings of disquiet and dire foreboding. We'd sit together on the ground, me against his sleek black body. We were equals then, fleas, dirt, spittle, smell and all.

Dogs were not equal at our house. Dickie was a yard dog; he was never permitted in the house. In summer he dug a cool hole under the floorboards; in the winter rain, he slept in our tool shed—if we remembered to leave the door open for him. He didn't get his dish washed regularly—there was usually a petrified grain of rice stuck to it; bones and corn cobs were thrown to him from the door. He often lay by the door waiting to get lucky, happy to be close to the sound of voices, even in pitched battle. His mother was a house dog and enjoyed the warmth and protection of a house in town and the company of lots of lonely and tired men. Oh sure, she got kicked now and then, but Dickie got that too.

I think I loved him most. My father was not an outwardly loving man, and my mother was too busy. My sister and brother were going on to more sophisticated interests. Dickie and I were always on the outside, panting to be let in, perfect for each other.

Dickie was with us through some of the worst years: the summer of my mother's pregnancy, the year our baby was born, and the time five months later when the baby drowned.

It was a very hot day, and we were at school. My mother had put our baby in a small tub of water—he loved water and would play contentedly in it for hours. She'd left him only a moment, she said, and he drowned in this small tub, in three inches of water on that hot September day.

That was the year of our disasters. Shortly after our baby died, our house burned to the ground. It was on a Sunday, December 13. My sister, my brother, and I were at the Buddhist church. And, though my brother was already driving (he was fourteen), he didn't take us directly home after the Japanese classes. Along about five o'clock, when there was hardly anyone left at the church, I asked him how come we weren't going home.

My sister said we had no home to go to. They hadn't told me anything until then. Later they said one of the incense sticks we burned at the tiny shrine for our baby fell and started the fire while we were at the church and our parents were in the fields.

We stayed at Mr. Nakamura's boardinghouse until my father and Mr. Ohira, who was a carpenter, built a two-bedroom house for us. It was a long building designed to be separated into units for easy loading onto truck beds when it came time to move. My mother said it was a costly house. Lumber workers were on strike, truckers were sympathizing, lumber prices were sky high, and everything had to be paid "cash in advance." I think the money came from the Buddhist community. They could always be counted on in death and dire need.

Dickie stayed at the ruins of the house during this time. My father took him table scraps from the boardinghouse when he could. Dickie drank from the pond as he always had and found the rest of his sustenance in the desert.

My mother was disconsolate with grief and guilt over the baby, the house, and life in general. She consulted a psychic from Los Angeles who told her to abide. He said things would change. A new baby would bring joy and love back to our grieving family. I waited for that magic time. It was a year, a month, and two weeks before the arrival of our baby sister. At last I could stop grieving.

The year that Hitler invaded Poland, my father went into partnership with a bachelor friend, and they leased 150 acres for a giant lettuce venture. Well, the bottom fell out of the lettuce market; it didn't even pay to harvest the crop. So acres and acres of overgrown lettuce lay withering in the fields. It was also the summer of the great Imperial Valley earthquake.

Everyone had gone to town that day, everyone but me. My brother was graduating from high school, and I suppose the excursion was for his new clothes. In the afternoon, along about three o'clock, the sky clouded over, and a strong wind blew in from the west. I felt strangely restless, so I took Dickie and walked among the furrows of dying lettuce, the wind snapping my skirt and tufting Dickie's short black hair. We were exhilarated by the wind, the dark sky, and the ghostly lettuce spikes.

When a real gale whipped up, I took Dickie into the house with me. This was the first time he'd ever been in the house. We huddled together on the floor until the family returned.

No one seemed unduly worried. My mother put together our supper, we ate, my sister's boyfriend dropped by, and, while my sister and I were doing the dishes, the earthquake struck.

My father yelled, "*Jishin da!*" It's an earthquake! We all scrambled out through the back door. Our tall pantry nearly fell on me, but the boyfriend held it up and we all got out safely. We could feel the earth move under the soles of our feet.

It continued to shake throughout the night. My mother sent my brother to the house for blankets and a lantern. Our ranch was across the road from the Augustas, a Portuguese family who owned their own land, pigs, turkeys, horses, cows, goats, and so on, and they could be heard hollering along with the cackling, mooing, and squealing of their animals. We had never socialized with them, although they sometimes gave us lard when they slaughtered pigs. My mother didn't know what to do with these large tubs of white fat. The road that ran between us separated us culturally, and we suffered the earthquake separate from them, isolated, except for my sister's boyfriend, who displayed a certain bravado.

We sat on the blankets, my sister's boyfriend and Dickie with us. Dickie did not leave my side for all my mother's nudging and pushing to keep him off the blankets. My father stood up suddenly and went into the house. I screamed for him to come back, but my mother said not to worry. She said these houses were accustomed to moving and shaking. "Just nails and wood. It'll sway and squeak, but it won't fall," she said.

My brother said dryly, "Lucky we're not rich."

"What do you mean?" I asked.

"Lucky we don't have a nice stucco house," he said. My sister's boyfriend snorted. My father came out with a glass and his jug of wine. My mother sighed deeply.

We slept outside that night, my sister's boyfriend lying closer to my brother than to her. Dickie was on a blanket with me, and my baby sister was in my mother's arms; she had her back to my father.

It was the combined force of the earthquake and the 150 acres of doomed lettuce that drove us out of the Imperial Valley. Other families left too, including the Nakamuras. It was a sort of Japanese exodus.

In Oceanside there was a village of Japanese working small cooperative farms, and there was work enough for our refugees. My sister and I left for Los Angeles earlier, my sister to attend junior college and I to spend the summer working as a mother's helper, cleaning, washing, and taking care of two cute blond girls for room and board and twenty-five dollars a month. My father gave Larry, the youngest Augusta boy, five dollars to look after Dickie until my father could decide what to do next.

When summer was over, I joined my family in Oceanside, but my sister stayed in Los Angeles. By early September, it was apparent we would not be returning to the valley. The Augustas asked us to take Dickie back, so my brother and I were appointed to return to Imperial for him. I was horrified that we were not to take him back with us to Oceanside. We'd never bucked our parents' tyranny, and it didn't occur to us to disobey them now. My brother told me we were the executioners.

Although Dickie was ecstatic to see us again, he seemed to know what was coming and wouldn't get into the car. We pushed and pulled and finally got him in and jumped in quickly before he could get out.

We drove out to the desert while Dickie paced in the back. I couldn't bring myself to sit with him to soothe him or even to turn around and look at him. Finally my brother drove back to the last place we had moved from, where our baby brother had drowned, where our house burned to the ground, where our little sister was born. There was nothing there except the old cottonwood tree and a shallow indentation of the pond. It didn't seem possible it had all happened in the two years of our lease or that traces of lives could be so quickly and silently erased. My brother said, "He knows this place. Maybe he'll have a fighting chance here."

Again Dickie balked. He didn't want to leave the car. We pushed and pulled and, as before, quickly jumped in and sped away.

I said good-bye in my heart because it seemed hypocritical to say it out loud. I couldn't speak to my brother, who was dealing with his own emotions. I watched Dickie run after us until the road turned. I prayed he would find his way back to the Augustas and that they, with kinder hearts than ours, would feed him, give him a drink, and pat him now and then.

That wasn't the last time I saw Dickie. For years he came to me in my dreams, always running, running to me. Sometimes I'm on a bus, sometimes in a stranger's car. Once his back appeared to be broken, but he continued to run. I am always watching him from a window, on a moving vehicle, my heart cut out of me.

We never returned to Imperial. Along with Dickie, we abandoned the house that cost so much, the refrigerator with its payments, a broken consul radio that didn't survive the earthquake, and probably some monstrous debts too.

We were in Oceanside when Japan attacked Pearl Harbor. During the war, despite our citizenship, we were incarcerated as enemy aliens, and after four years in camp and through many agonizing choices, our family splintered and took off in different directions. My sister left for Arkansas (with a clearance) to marry a soldier. My brother chose expatriation and was shipped off to another camp in Northern California and waited to be deported. He had refused to defend a country that would put its loyal citizens in a concentration camp. I relocated to Chicago. Only my father, mother, and little sister were left in camp.

Shortly after the bombing of Hiroshima, camps were ordered to close. My father became very ill and died of bleeding ulcers a week before the final closure. My brother was not deported, and eventually we got together in San Diego.

Somehow we lived through this tumultuous period, nomads again, outwardly whole, but no one was unscarred. Still we found people to love and marry.

My husband and I married at the start of the Korean War. His father hadn't approved of me, he wanted a more compliant daughter-in-law, a more traditional Nisei woman for his son, but when the draft was reinstated and young unmarried men started leaving for Korea, he hastily put together a wedding for us. We were married by a Buddhist priest in my husband's brother's house. In our twenty-five years of marriage , we had one child, Joy.

My husband was a kind and indulgent father. He gave Joy anything she asked for: goldfish, chicks, hamsters, a turtle who fell out of his dish and disappeared. Years later I found him under a dresser. He had died silently in our bedroom, dehydrating in agony while we slept, made love, made war. There were also two cats named Sukey, and there was Freckles, Joy's first dog, a Dalmation.

He was a cute puppy, but we had to put him out in the yard when he grew so quickly. He was hyperactive, tenacious, and had a sense of humor that wouldn't quit. He chewed all the reachable clothes drying on the line. I watched him from my kitchen window and ran out with a broom every time he sidled up to the laundry. Then he'd hang his head, lie down, pretend abject humility, and would wait patiently for me to leave the window before he dashed about wreaking havoc again. He chewed off leather collars, easily popped chain leashes, dug holes under the fence, and ran away for even greater adventures. He terrorized the neighborhood kids, knocking them off their feet and standing over them, nudging them down when they tried to get up. His affection was relentless; he pounced on us, drooling, licking, and piddling with unrestrained joy.

When I put down his supper, I first threw out a stick (we kept a supply by the back door) and called out, "Fetch!" When he tore out to fetch, I put down his huge dinner and quickly backed into the house. He joyfully accepted this routine as part of the dinner ritual and waited far back in the yard for my stick.

I stopped hanging over the back fence with my neighbor because Freckles constantly clawed, gnawed, chewed every available surface and joint, and salivated over it all, tearing my clothes and ruining my shoes. I screamed and threatened and sometimes even tried to ignore him. Then he'd back off and take a running leap at me, throwing me to the ground and knocking the wind out of me.

Mr. Reubens, my mother-in-law's neighbor, offered to take Freckles off our hands. He claimed he knew how to handle Freckles' kind. He already had two dogs and was married to a silent and sour woman who usually let him have his way. I suppose he just wore her down with his persistence and endless cheer. He was a lot like Freckles.

Within a week Reubens was complaining that Freckles had barked all night, every night, and, when he brought him into the house, Freckles hopped into bed with his big old stinky self and stood over his wife and wouldn't let her up. He said Freckles would flip women's skirts—church women, his wife's friends, he chortled—and then he'd sprint away. He told my mother-in-law that Freckles was not trainable. An impossible dog. He said that in desperation he took Freckles to Mount Baldy and abandoned him there.

Shades of Dickie! But I was not surprised at anything humans might do to animals. It would be Reuben's dreams that Freckles would haunt, not mine. My husband, who as a boy was never permitted a dog, was shocked. He was a gentle though unyielding man. He was prepared to look for Freckles wherever Mount Baldy was. He didn't know.

It turned out Reubens was only joking, trying to scare my prim mother-in-law. "Why," he laughed, "I wouldn't do that to my wife, much less my dog," he said.

My brother-in-law, husband of my little sister, loved dogs and would sometimes come to play with Freckles. This was before they had their five children. He said Freckles should be out in the open fields chasing rabbits, and we were doing a terrible injustice keeping him in the city without freedom, without affection. My brother-in-law found a friend, a farmer, whose heart was bigger, whose life was larger, who could accommodate Freckles' enormous affection, appreciate his great sense of humor, and who—this is important—owned a washer-dryer.

Our daughter Joy had Lucky after Freckles. Lucky was a smaller dog, a mixture of terrier, Chihuahua, toy poodle, and whatever else. Joy named him Lucky because my brother's family had adopted one from the same litter that quickly perished, and ours, being so small, needed to be lucky to survive. He was lucky all right; he was always with Joy, eating from her bag of chips, sleeping with her winter and summer under the covers in the airless pocket at her feet. He was the only one who truly knew Joy. She was a secretive child.

Lucky was smart. I quickly trained him to sit, speak. and roll over, but he developed a rash from the stress, and we all agreed he shouldn't have to do tricks and that we should accept him as a dog just as he accepted us as nondogs. The neighborhood kids teased him mercilessly through the wire fence, and he spent much of his day rushing back and forth along the fence, barking and snarling. He had no sense of humor; he distrusted white and black kids, grew to be quite racist, tolerating only Japanese kids, most of them Joy's gentle cousins. From her father's side.

We moved to a larger place in Gardena. which before World War II was a community of Japanese farmers. Long before that, with a Spanish governor, much of the area was given in huge land grants to Spanish settlers from Mexico. The Spanish wanted to secure California territory before the Russian fur traders claimed it. Many townships, to this day, have Spanish-Mexican names: El Segundo, Dominguez Hills, Hermosa Beach, Redondo, for example. The Japanese residents left during the war, forced into the camps, and rural Gardena made way for enormous defense factories and subdivision tract homes, which sprouted like mushrooms on abandoned farms.

By the time we moved to Gardena, the big war had been over for some twenty years, defense industries were gone, and with Japan's defeat, trade with the United States exploded and Japan established huge offices and warehouses in outlying areas. Gardena still had remnants of her old provinciality; a few frame houses still stood their ground but were fast disappearing. Even the relatively new tract homes were giving way to apartments and condominiums.

We found a lovely house with a pool—the only reason Joy would move. The backyard was enclosed on three sides by a five-foot cinder block wall. Lucky hated it. He spent most of his time on Joy's bed looking out the window that faced the street. He watched the kids walking to and from school, but they hardly noticed the little brown dog looking out to them, waiting to be teased.

Every night he'd wait until we were asleep and then pee on our brand new couch. Not on the floor, not against the wall, not by the door, but on our green faux-silk sofa. Every morning I'd carry him to the couch, push his nose in the pee stain, hit him with a rolled up sheet of paper, and holler, "No! No!" as if he didn't understand.

One morning he saw me coming, the rolled up paper raised, screaming my personal best. Apparently this was it, he'd had it. He snarled and bit me, his teeth just grazing my knuckles. Joy yelled, "Leave him alone!"

After that we came to a truce. I left him alone, and he stopped soiling the couch. I still don't understand the logic of it.

At this time my husband's catering business was enjoying a modest success, and he began accumulating stuff his parents never allowed him: a dog of his own, a motorcycle, a van, leather pants and jacket, and some up-to-date threads. His personal dog was Sport, a pedigreed German Shepherd, who Lucky-the-mutt resented with a passion.

Sport quickly grew three times Lucky's size, but Lucky claimed seniority, ceaselessly growling and snapping at Sport. Sport good-naturedly tolerated most of this, but one day he was pushed to the edge, and he grabbed Lucky by the neck, shaking him big time, fully intending to break Lucky's neck.

After that we separated them. Lucky in the side yard and Sport in the back. My husband found Tigger abandoned in a churchyard, and Tigger shared the back space with Sport. Tigger was a tiny waif that my husband swore would remain small. "Look at his tiny paws," he said, and indeed they were small, but Tigger grew at least as large as Sport and as energetic and hairy to boot. No amount of soap washed away that look of disorder and dishevelment. But he had the best nature of the three dogs. Or of all of us.

With financial success came estrangement. My husband found people who were more exciting, who could give more to him, more freely. It was a form of enlightenment for both of us: painful, nevertheless a learning experience and freedom from old concepts—one man, one woman, a nuclear family.

When he left us, he took Sport with him. Actually I insisted because Sport needed to be walked, brushed, and otherwise attended to; too much for me to handle along with the emotional distress and a reproachful Joy. Besides, Sport missed his master.

Sport was trained to respond to every command immediately (like a good German soldier). After the divorce, my husband often took him to the hills of Griffith Park and let him run free. One day my husband called, "Come!" Sport heard him and obeyed. It was dusk and neither of them saw the car rounding the treacherous curves of the park road. Sport died in my husband's van, on his girlfriend's lap, as they were taking him to the vet. My husband said it was my fault; I shouldn't have insisted that he take Sport with him.

My little sister, her husband, and their five children had moved to Santa Barbara, so it was not my brother-in-law who found a home for our Tigger. A childless Nisei couple in their senior years needed a dog to protect them, and Tigger was recommended by a friend. Joy and I scrubbed him down and hoped the couple would like him. They did. They fell in love with him. They were so happy, they returned later with gifts: a twenty-five-pound bag of rice and a tin of Japanese crackers.

After I pulled myself together somewhat, Isadora joined us as Lucky's bride. She was a small wild thing with curly orange hair that Joy cut to look like a lion's mane. Lucky loved his dancing bride. In his old age, he fathered four puppies, one of them stillborn. Isadora gave birth under my bed. Joy's friend Pam, who was visiting that day, took the stillborn pup that neither Joy nor could get ourselves to touch, and tenderly put her in a sock for us. We buried her under the persimmon tree.

We gave the other pups away. Two to a family who already had three dogs. The other, a cute puppy with short brown hair, went to a young man who called the dog Sushi because he looked like the sushi made of a pocket of fried tofu stuffed with rice.

Soon after weaning the pups, Isadora found the back gate unlocked and ran away. We waited and called and made the rounds of animal shelters, but she never returned to us. Lucky was always racing out unclosed doors, but he wasn't so young or fleet that we couldn't catch him. But there was one time he sneaked out and worried us for weeks.

We scoured the neighborhood and the shelters before and after school each day to no avail. After a couple of weeks we decided to make one final trip to the shelter. If we couldn't find him, we agreed to trust that Lucky was in a better place. This trip was also fruitless. Joy hardly spoke to me on the ride home. As we drove up the driveway, we could see Lucky waiting for us at the front door. He was already too old to show much emotion, and Joy has never been subject to excesses, so she just clasped him tightly and buried her face in his soiled fur while he looked at me with his rheumy eyes.

Lucky appeared tired and sad, as though his quest had been unsuccessful. Maybe he was looking for Isadora. Maybe someone had picked him up hoping to keep him but found him too cantankerous or too old. Or maybe he had escaped from another untended door. Heck, while we're at it, we can believe that he really did find Isadora, but after a brief reunion, she went back to her second husband and family. It was a far, far better thing that he did return to us.

We took Lucky to the veterinarian when he could no longer jump curbs. We thought it was either his eyes or his legs. It was both. Then his kidneys failed, and there were more medicines, and finally the doctor said by dog years Lucky was already 119; and, if he were human, we might consider putting him in a convalescent home and medicating him, but this was a sick and miserable dog, and we should let him go quietly to that long sleep. It was the kind thing to do, he said.

That was all. The assistant to the doctor held Lucky while the doctor administered the hypodermic. He said Lucky would just drift off to sleep. The assistant asked if we cared to hold Lucky until then.

"No-no," we both said quickly. Cowards again. Lucky looked at us with his sad eyes until we turned our backs and closed the door.

On the way home, Joy said, "We should have held him. Then he would know he was safe."

"Yes, we should have held him," I said.

"We let him down."

"Yes, we let him down." I was the mother. Why didn't I do the right thing? Afraid of commitment. Afraid of intimacy. Afraid of trust.

For months at night, I would hear Lucky running through the foyer, his nails clipping along the tile floor. Joy heard him too. His pace is spirited; he has come back to us young again. And for years I've seen his sad eyes looking at me as when we turned our backs on him at the vet's, like Dickie, running, running, his eyes never leaving me, while I stand above, in a bus, in a car, looking back, heartless. Will I always look back in regret?

Well, it's too late now anyway. Too late for making up or counting up or trying to balance the ledger. And life habits are hard to shake. They are, as my mother said, only *keda mono*, only animals. Only dogs. It's hard enough for humans to survive in this uncaring world. Who are dogs to ask for more than we do?

But that's what they're born into: a simple life with simple rewards, a warm pat, a kind word. Such a life without complex motives is tempting, but it's too late to change now. I'll hold that margin wide. I will not let them come into my house and break my heart. And I will not break their hearts again. I will not let them trust me again.

So don't come to me, stinky dog, with your bad breath, your fleas, your warm saliva, your sad eyes, and needs I can't fulfill. I'm not your keeper. Don't count on me.

It's the autumn of my days; I feel the chill breath of winter. Do not trust me to look after you. And if luck is with us, we may meet again in another spring.

Pain and Stuff

I saw Maisie around in the internment camp; she was maybe fourteen or fifteen, a couple of years younger than I was. She was named Masako; her family called her "Masa," her contemporaries "Massie," and finally "Maisie" after the beloved ditzy character Ann Southern played on screen. Our Maisie was cute, giggly, and superficial, or so I thought.

After our liberation from internment at the end of World War II, we often ran into one another in Japanese enclaves that were quickly reestablished or at the workplaces that hired Japanese. We were both Nisei, the first generation of American born. I found Maisie in a downtown warehouse where many of us Nisei girls filled orders (during department store sales) for rich white families: a case of two-ply toilet paper, half a dozen sets of Fieldcrest towels, a dozen cakes of designer soap, and cases of creams and jellies and other youth-preserving ointments. They go back a long way.

I met Maisie again at a stationery factory. We tied dainty bundles of pastel paper and matching envelopes with gauzy ribbons. I remembered the white woman who was the champion bow maker there—at it fifteen years. She rocked in her seat as she worked. I thought, "Holy Moley, fifteen years in the same chair, rocking away, tying the same bows." Fifteen years seemed like an eternity then. She didn't like me; I suppose it was my attitude and the fact that I almost beat her record in the third week I was there. It was only a matter of getting the right rhythm; any moron could have done it. (Years later Maisie reminded me that I had said that. I was pretty arrogant then.) Maisie and I did not socialize outside of work.

About then I met a young Nisei guy who was attending UCLA.

The hormones were running rampant and we fell for each other big time, and against our better judgment, we married. While he went for his degree, I worked, again at factory production. He sold insurance after graduating, and we moved to Gardena, a community of Japanese Americans a few miles southwest of Los Angeles. My husband's business was with Nisei; insurance is big with us; you can scare us with any threat of economic, political, or natural disaster. Few of us cared to buck the restrictive covenant barring minorities from white residential areas, so again we gathered in communities in the outskirts: Gardena, Torrance, Monterey Park, Montebello. We were hard working, competitive, and wary—the expect-nothing, say-little, hope-for-the-best Nisei.

Maisie had also moved to Gardena. Sometimes we'd see each other at a supermarket. We always nodded to one another. Once we talked long enough for me to understand that she had married a man she met at a Nisei dance class. He was now a chiropractor. That's the way I understood it. She worked in a garment factory until his business got on its feet, and now, of course, she no longer had to work but she still did. "I don't know," she said. "I guess I'm kind of insecure."

Once we chatted briefly before she rushed off to beauty school; she was preparing to become a beautician. "Good for you," I said enviously. I wished there was an attainable goal I could put my energy toward—a job where I wouldn't have to spend long hours on my feet. But it was okay. I didn't really need to work. We didn't need the money—well, not that much. I had a family to take care of; I had convinced myself it was a noble job.

A few years later we met again at a supermarket. She told me then she had three children. That was possible, I thought, but she'd never spoken of them before. I said, "My, how time does fly! Three kids? You know, I never thought of you as being the mother type—you know, the big lap, cooking and sewing, wiping noses, changing diapers type." I had only one daughter.

They were not her children, she said. Her husband was a widower. She stayed at home now. She had quit her job at the hair salon to care for the family, she said. The youngest, Alan, was four when his mother died. Maisie married Fred soon after. "I think he was looking for someone to take care of his kids. It's pretty hard for a man with three motherless children, you know," Maisie giggled. For a split second the old Maisie flashed through.

I laughed with her, but my mind was ticking away: she had met this man at a dance some years ago, and he was already a widower with three kids. Maisie, who could have had any man she fluttered her lashes at, fell for a man with a family. "Boy, he must have something else besides a bunch of kids," I said aloud.

Well, it wasn't her first marriage, Maisie said. The first one, she'd met at a dance. It didn't work out.

"The chiropractor, right?" I asked.

"No," she laughed. She looked at her watch. "I have to run," she said.

Strange, I thought. There were unconnected frames, jumps and starts, and I wanted to tidy up this story. But okay; if Maisie didn't care to explain, I could live with it. Heck, I hardly knew her. I didn't tell her about my life either. In fact, I hardly told her anything. Well, I'd said I had a daughter. And a husband. And that he sold insurance—all types: health, car, property, fire, flood, earthquake (he asked me to spread the word). I didn't feel the pain of her divorce because I had no experience in that area. In fact, very few Nisei were divorced. It just wasn't done at that time. We always put on the best face: our children were smart or smart enough, our incomes were adequate or better, our husbands reliable and faithful. Oh, sure.

When Maisie and I first started to meet regularly, we were middle-aged. She still looked good. She'd gone back to work, part time, taking appointments from friends. She would cut my hair once a month or so, and sometimes we'd have lunch together.

We didn't talk about anything of substance; her Alan was in high school; the other two had moved out of the house, the girl to Oregon and the boy to New York.

"Well, congratulations," I said. "You did it! You brought them up and sent them on their way."

"Just one more to go," she laughed.

Like Alan, my daughter was in her last year of high school. When I asked her about Alan, she said they didn't move in the same circles. She knew who he was but, "well," she said, "Alan's a loner." She told me she saw him around campus mostly smooching with his girlfriend. "He's an awesome looking dude," she said.

"Oh yeah? What's he look like?" I asked.

"Well, like…well, moody. Like James Dean. He's smart too. Does all of Susan's homework. When he's not smooching with her, he's working on her homework. Cigarette dangling from his mouth and scowling, you know, like a movie star."

She knew a lot about him for someone who didn't move in the same circles. So he was a good-looking dude. I got the picture: A curl of smoke clouding his vision, a slight squint, maybe a lock of hair falling over his brow, like a movie star. They all smoked then; it was the ultimate in sophistication. Drugs hadn't entered the high school scene yet. Not hard drugs. Well, what did I know?

"Smoking?" I asked. "I wonder if his parents know about it."

"He doesn't care. He doesn't care who knows it."

"It looks to me like he's trying awfully hard to grow up," I said.

My daughter sighed patiently. "Everyone is," she said.

"Well don't try too hard. You'll be grown up a long, long time, and you'll wish many times you were in high school again." That was a lie. I was turning into my mother, saying things that sounded good but had no truth in them. I'd never wished I were in high school again. Never felt part of my high school. About the time kids were talking senior prom, we were whisked off to the camps, where all West Coast Japanese and Japanese Americans were herded. Four years in camp; four more years out, scrambling from one crummy job to another. Where had my youth gone? What happened to the carefree years? Was I ever happy? Sure, I was. Remember love and motherhood? I've had my share. Maybe more than my share, given my neurotic nature. But after each feast, a hunger returned and hung around like a recurring dream. What did I want? But I'm drifting.

"When he's not alone, he's with Susan," my daughter said. "If Susan dropped him, there'd be ten girls waiting in line. I mean *today;* you know? And not just Japanese girls," she said.

"You among them?" I asked.

"Naw," she said. "Not my type. Too serious. A guy doesn't have to be that good-looking, you know, and, for sure, not that serious. I like someone with a little sense of humor. Not like a clown, you know, but more fun. No one messes with Mr. Alan 'cuz he's got a real temper. Flares up like a firecracker. 'Have Gun, Will Travel', you know what I mean? Stay out of his way, Dude. And everybody does. That's why he's a loner."

"Does he actually fight?"

"Doesn't have to, much. His reputation, you know. That's all he needs. No one messes with him anymore."

"A smoocher too, huh?"

"Yeah, a real lover boy. And a smoker. Smokes like a chimney."

"Won't they expel him for that?"

"Doesn't get caught, I guess."

"Smooching and smoking and getting away with it. And smart too."

"You got it. A smart smooching smoker. Solitary too," she added, rounding out the *s*'s.

"Alan lost his mother when he was four," I reminded her. "That's a lot of lonely years he's endured."

"Lots of people lose their mothers, but they're not all loners," my daughter said. She had me there.

Of course, I never told Maisie any of this. Yet, I thought, if I were a true friend, wouldn't I tell her what was happening at school? It was shocking to me, but maybe this was normal for the times. It's not my business anyway. Well, Alan will soon be out of school. and he'll grow up. He'll be off to college. And probably he'll be smooching and smoking on another campus with another girl.

It *wasn't* my business. I should respect Maisie's privacy. I don't like people trying to fix things for *me*. I don't want people nosing around in *my* life. What if she were to tell me what to do with *my* problem. I'd tell her to butt out. Well no, I wouldn't do that. We Nisei women are notoriously polite.

I'd probably do what my husband usually does when he's put on the defensive. He gets on the offense. I'd learned a thing or two from the years I'd spent with him. I'd ask her why she got out of her first marriage; how bad was it? I'd remind her that all relationships have ups and downs; she'd know that. The thing is to ride the rough times out—ride it out. *Gambare,* which means gather the troops. Resist. Dig in. Fight the good fight. There are bad years in everyone's life—every marriage. Just work past one more hurdle, then everything will be all right, and no one would be wiser and we'd be like everyone else, happy and successful. Just one more smile, one more mile.

Maisie said one day, "You know, my Nisei ladies (she called us her 'ladies') all seem to have such great lives. They all seem happy. Nobody complains about husbands or children, or money, or anything. Everybody's happy. Everything's great. Isn't that something?"

I said, "Is that so?"

"Yeah. You'd never think they had a problem in the world. Marriages made in heaven, plenty of money, great kids.... Would you believe it?"

I felt a rush of adrenaline. She's trying to draw me out. Maybe she'd heard something. Maybe people were talking. Maybe I was the so-called last to know. Is she trying to tell me something?

Well, sure he was out almost every night. Till late. That's the nature of his business—taking up the pitfalls of life, twisting arms. Every night? Well, sure people work during the day. Night's the only free time left. Nights are better. Clients are tired, less resistant. What does she know?

Maybe he was seen leaving a motel, a floozy on his arm. No. That wouldn't happen. He's too fastidious. It would have to be a serious relationship. Not just anyone. Still, we were bickering and quarreling all the time. One disagreement trailed into another. There were no more apologies, not even a half-hearted "I'm sorry, but if you hadn't done blah-blah, then I wouldn't have said blah-blah." No wiping off the slate and starting a fresh quarrel on another day. There was no caring, no tenderness. Still, I think I had hope because outside I made a huge effort to feign normalcy. While I smiled and put up a front, everyone whispered and surmised. What an embarrassment.

"All Nisei can't be that happy, can they?" Maisie asked.

"Happy, happy, who's happy?" That's it, make it light. "Maybe if we don't ask for too much, we could all be happy," I said. "We have even more than our parents had. We have decent homes, a fair livelihood, pretty good kids, good friends. Our parents worked harder and had less and then lost it all (the incarceration, you remember). Isn't that 'happy' enough?"

"You think so?" She put her fingers through my hair. "You know, one of my ladies found her son hanging in the garage."

I gasped. Suicide? I was not expecting this. I had my dialogue ready for the pitch, and Maisie threw me a curve. I thought of the poor mother who, like myself, had smiled daily while her heart was breaking. Maybe she too believed time would pass and before anyone was aware, everything would straighten itself out. *Gaman* is the Japanese word for enduring. It has the sense of suffering and outlasting the condition.

"Yet," Maisie continued, "you'd never know by looking at her. She's always so cheerful. She talked about church, her friends, her vacations...never anything about her son. Do you think she didn't know he had problems?"

"Well, I don't know," I said. I always watched myself in Maisie's chair. All those scalp massages could loosen the tongue, could open up the tear ducts. Pity is not a good thing to want. I asked Maisie, "Would you tell people about your problems?"

"I guess not," she said.

My divorce was painful but quick. I decided to face the storm head-on and very simply told anyone who asked, "He left me." Most people let it go at that, but some asked for particulars. I said, "One day he picked up his clothes and left." My daughter was devastated, but she carried on with the spunk she'd always shown. It's part of the heritage. No whining, no pleading, just a lot of internal hemorrhaging.

Maisie was sympathetic. "Oh, gee, I didn't know at all. You never said anything."

"That's the way we are," I said.

"Oh, yeah, I know that." There was a long silence. "What are you going to do now?"

"Find a job, I guess. Carry on. What else is there?" Suddenly one of the quick frames of Maisie's life flashed at me. I said, "I know now how hard it must have been for you." Our eyes met in the mirror, but she looked blank. "Your first husband," I said. She measured a lock of hair.

"The chiropractor," I reminded.

"I'd like to try another cut today, is that okay?"

"Okay," I said, but I couldn't let it go. "It's terrible, but it looks like we can only relate to one another through our own experience. Maybe you really have to get hurt before you can empathize," I said.

"Yes," she said, "the first one really hurt. But he wasn't the chiropractor. After my divorce, I was with a couple of other guys. The chiropractor was one of them. That hurt too, but you got to move on or... or..."

"Hang in the garage."

"Yeah," she said. And, "Oh, God!" She sighed deeply as she wiped her eyes with my towel.

"Gee, I didn't mean to sound so...so callous. It just came out that way," I said.

"That's okay," she said. Then she told me she was planning to work from her home. "Now that two of the kids are gone, I have lots of space. I'll fix up one of their rooms, install a sink, tables, a big mirror, you know."

"The works, huh, Maisie?"

"Yeah. I'll even serve tea and cookies. Next time, you'll be coming to the house for your cut."

I met Alan at the house one Saturday. My daughter was right; he was handsome and not only silent—he was morose. I wondered why Maisie would subject Alan to the coming and going of her "ladies" when we were an obvious intrusion. But I didn't say anything. Maisie brought it up first. She said, "Ignore him. He's going through a phase."

"He doesn't like us here, does he?" I said.

"He'll get over it," Maisie said.

After she heard him slam the door and speed off in his car, Maisie checked her "lady" under the drier and said to me, "I had to quit working at the salon because Alan was cutting classes. The school called and told me he was cutting classes."

"Is everything all right now?" I asked.

"Yeah, more or less," she said. That was all she said at that session.

The next time I had an appointment, more of it came out: Alan had been bringing Susan to the house while everyone was out. One day Maisie came home unexpectedly and found them.

"I thought the school called you," I said, trying to look detached.

"Yeah, they did," she said. "That was about cutting classes. This is something else."

"Well maybe it isn't what you think," I said.

"It's worse. They were doing it. I don't know how long it's been going on; he won't say. Well, my husband and I went to talk with Susan's parents, and that's when we found out they just hate him. They despise him. They said they'd call the police if he ever came near Susan again."

"What are you going to do? You can't follow them around. You can't keep them apart."

"I know that. When my husband said I had to quit my job and be home, I didn't know what to do. I love doing hair. It's what's kept me sane all these years. Oh, it's been hard. You don't know how hard it's been. That boy, from the beginning, just hated me. Four years old. Tantrums all the time with the screaming and kicking. The whole enchilada. I couldn't get near him. Wouldn't let me touch him. He didn't want *me*. He wanted his mother. But his mother was dead. She couldn't come back to him.

"Actually, none of them liked me, but the older ones, you know, it was easier for them because I made the meals and washed the clothes and cleaned the house, you know. And eventually they accepted me, but that one, Alan, he's stubborn. I just couldn't reach him.

"It was hard, God, it was hard, but I had to make it work because, you know, I just couldn't keep … keep changing partners all my life. I had to make it work. I just had to." Then she said, "Or that's what I thought. Maybe it would have been better just to stay single and make my own way."

"Who knows?" What else could I say?

It was late summer the next time I went to Maisie. My daughter had graduated and was getting ready to attend a college nearby. Most of her friends were enrolled in big universities out of state. I guess it was hard for her to leave home. I think it was the divorce. I told Maisie maybe my daughter was still hoping we'd get back together again, but that was a long shot because her father was in a serious relationship with someone. Maisie said I was lucky to have a girl of my own who loved me enough to want to stay close by. Well, I knew that.

"What's Alan doing now?" I asked.

"Oh, Alan," Maisie sighed. "I guess I might as well tell you," she said. "Alan was involved with this girl, you know. They were really in it deep, and my husband went to talk to the girl's parents and they just put a stop to it. They watched her like a hawk. Well, she was only sixteen, you know, and they didn't want anything to happen, you know what I mean? They wouldn't let him near her."

I wondered if Susan was pregnant. That would be the absolute worse scenario for a Nisei parent at that time. Next to hanging in the garage. It would shame the whole family. "What about school," I asked. "Don't they see each other at school?"

"They took her out and sent her to a private school. One day Alan went to their house, but they wouldn't let him in. He screamed like a maniac, they said. He called out for her over and over, but she wouldn't go to him. He kicked down the back door and broke windows. The whole neighborhood came out to watch. They called the police, the parents did. It was horrible. We had to bail him out.

"Well, you know, you can't keep two people who love each other apart. So in desperation they sent the girl out of state to live with relatives. I don't blame them, but it was terrible to watch Alan. He had no money, no job; he couldn't run away with her—couldn't call her or even see her. There was nothing he could do. I could see it was tearing him up, but...well, what could we do? The parents hated him.

"And in court the judge told Alan it was either jail or two years in the army. We couldn't let him go to jail. What would people say?"

Poor Alan. I saw him raising his fist to the gray sky and calling out to Susan, walking the desolate streets like Heathcliff on the moors, his movie star face in a black scowl, the heart beneath his fluttering shirt breaking. But Alan was still a boy. He was powerless. He couldn't even get drunk. When I was able to speak, I said, "So he's in the army then."

"Yeah," Maisie said. "He comes home now and then and stays in his room most of the time."

"How sad," I said.

"Well, sometimes he drives off somewhere. We don't ask him where he's been. After all, he's almost a man now. He's entitled to his privacy. But he's feeling better, I think. He's getting used to it. He's all right."

Getting used to heartbreak? He's all right? "It seems like the boy is programmed for abandonment." I guess I said it aloud.

"You think so?" Maisie asked.

"No, not really," I said.

"She wrote to him over here, you know," Maisie said. "The girl. Her parents told us to destroy her letters, but I didn't have the heart. I sent them on to Alan. To the Marine base. I think he wrote to her too, but they, you know, the relatives, I'm sure they threw his letters out."

"Really?"

"Yeah, he told me," Maisie nodded. "She kept begging him to write, and after a while she stopped. Stopped writing. She thinks he's forgotten her. And there was nothing he could do. Couldn't even call her."

Two years pass quickly even when the days themselves are long.

The army did Alan a lot of good. He put on weight and got a healthy tan, and all that brutal training left little time or energy to obsess on Susan. Other soldiers took a liking to this too quiet, too solitary kid. Alan reenlisted for two more years.

The army also sent him to school, and by the time the last two years passed, Alan had a great job waiting for him. Computer programming, Maisie said proudly.

Alan moved immediately into his own apartment and went to work. Some weekends he had dinner with Fred and Maisie. One day he brought Debra with him. They were living together.

"She's a real floozy. Not Japanese," Maisie said. "Anyway, when she went to his car for something, I said, 'Why her, Alan? You can do better than that,' and, you know, he said, 'Well, Mom, she had no place to go.' So he did find her on the streets then. Geez, I'm glad he's kindhearted, but there's a limit, don't you think? Then I said maybe he should try to find Susan again. He said he'd heard she'd married a white guy back east."

Debra brought back a bottle of wine, and the two of them sat drinking and smoking and tittering all afternoon in Maisie's kitchen. "They could have done that at their own place," Maisie complained.

It was months before she called Alan. "My husband said to leave them alone," Maisie said, "but I was really worried, so I called him. And, you know, a woman answered the phone, so I asked, "Debra?"

The woman said no but wouldn't give her name. Maisie asked for Alan.

"He's not home yet," the woman was brusque.

"Well, tell him his Mom called," Maisie said. She wondered about the gal calling Alan's place "home." Not that she would have asked, but Alan didn't return the call anyway.

At that time, Maisie asked me, "What is he doing? He blames us for what happened with his girlfriend, and he's trying to punish us. But it wasn't our fault. Fred says to leave the boy alone; he has to live his own life; we can't interfere any more. 'No more,' he said, 'the boy has to do what's right for himself.' But I told him that can't be right; he's ruining his life."

After that Maisie stopped talking about Alan altogether. And I didn't ask about him.

A few years passed. Early one morning, just hours before my appointment, Maisie called to cancel. "We have to go to Ventura to help

Alan. He's sick and can't get out of bed," she said. "I'll call when I get back and make another date, okay?"

But I didn't hear from her for days, and then weeks, and when the month was over, I called her. "How's Alan?" I asked.

"He's in the hospital; he's dying," Maisie said. "I'm sorry I didn't call you back, but we've been so busy. Doctor told us to prepare, you know? We paid his bills and cleaned out his apartment; he didn't have much. The woman just cleared out. Just left a lot of empty bottles and dirty dishes. He's in terrible pain." And then, "Maybe you ought to find another beautician," she said. Dear Maisie—always thinking of her "ladies."

Alan died not long after that. It was the big C. "So young to have cancer," I said. "Wouldn't you have guessed it with all that smoking?" my daughter said. She talks like that when she tries to hide her feelings.

We went to the funeral together, my daughter and I. Some of her high school classmates were there, looking like a bevy of models in chic black. They let out little squeals of recognition. My daughter waved her fingers but didn't join them.

I wouldn't have thought there'd be so many people. There were the Sansei (third-generation Japanese American) classmates, but Alan's more recent friends were white, Chicano, a few blacks, and a sprinkling of girls. No floozies. No Susan, my daughter said.

I think Alan's friends were surprised at the Buddhist ceremony. They walked to the coffin, bowed their heads and put their hands together, took a pinch of incense, and sprinkled it in the smoldering burner just the way they saw us Japanese do. There were three priests in ornate robes— layers of rich brocade and silk—chanting long prayers, striking brass gongs, and stroking their prayer beads. There were a lot of us gray-haired old folk there. Friends of the family.

The young folk marched glumly by. They were feeling their mortality. Maybe they were thinking, "Why Alan? Why not one of them?" meaning us. Some of us were nodding off like it was just another dull television show. It's true: we'd had our turn. And it's true: we should have gone before Alan.

I thought he would look wasted with the ravages of the disease, but the mortuary did an excellent job. He looked too good, too young to die. His head rested on an ivory satin pillow, tented under a gossamer veil.

A secret smile played on his movie-star face—as though he were having the last laugh after all. There was no evidence of the devastating losses he'd endured in his short life. Or maybe all that had transpired was only a prelude to the next phase. Or maybe the smile was just a mortician's flourish on a slow day, and beneath the handsome suit lay the real Alan, beyond our cruel reach.

That was some time ago. Now, of course, we have all grown old, and Maisie accommodates only a few of her "Nisei ladies"—those of us who can still get around on our own steam. We repeat ourselves, repeat one another, nodding and affirming each sentence, compare physical problems, pretend to hear more than we do. Old heartaches, like old scars, have faded; only old stories (told with snorts of bravado) keep them alive. Few regrets remain.

Annie Hall, Annie Hall

Another Saturday night, another night of revelry.

Just kidding. It's just one more weekend night. I've spent a lot of these alone with my faithful TV—the one in the bedroom, not the one in the front room that Jeff, my son-in-law installed for me with all the up-to-the-minute stuff (of the time). The DVD is now a couple of years old (my grandkids love it), and the VCR is practically expiring from old age and neglect. The satellite dish is still fairly new. Jeff bought it originally for his own mother, but she didn't want it since all the programs are in English and her first and almost only language is Japanese.

After his mother rejected the satellite dish, Jeff installed it on my roof. He also bought me another TV to accommodate a DVD. I am past declining any gift, large or small. I'm grateful.

That TV with all its accessories is in a small built-in cabinet designed for technologies of another era. My house is old, but Jeff found a set with almost the exact dimensions of the small cabinet. He and Faith (my daughter) very nearly mangled his hands fitting it in. It could have been disastrous since Jeff needs his hands (and who doesn't?). He's a dentist.

There is a smaller TV in my bedroom without all the gadgetry (except for the remote). I usually watch this one because I can lie down in relative comfort and even doze a bit while the shows drone on. And on.

The sleep button is a godsend, but I recently lost the remote. How do you lose a remote? Easily, if you're as forgetful as I am. I've looked everywhere: under the bed, under the dresser and in its nine drawers, on the night table (and in its drawer), in the deep folds of the recliner. I've torn the bed apart, looked through my closet among the lint balls in the shoe boxes (mine congregate with a passion), and I've even looked in the fridge.

The other night I sat on the recliner, disgusted with the TV and all that getting up to change the channels and up again to lower the sound (during commercials) and up and down, up and down. I finally turned it off, threw a "FORGET YOU!" over my shoulder, and went to the other TV.

I chose to watch *Annie Hall* on satellite. *Annie Hall* is pretty old, but I hadn't seen it when it was first run and I was younger and could keep up with the youthful antics of white people. It claimed to be a three-star comedy, and I needed the laughs. Badly.

The front room TV is a little low for me, and I can't get a good angle lying on the couch or sitting on a chair, so I did what the kids do: I pulled down a couple of cushions and lay on the floor. I got comfortable one way or another, but after settling down, I noticed a layer of dust (now at eye level) on the dark tile of the dining room floor, and, being a neat freak (the kids say), I thought I'd just swab a damp mop over it while the host was doing the introduction thing for *Annie Hall*. After that, what would I be able to miss?

I did hear him say it was one of the finest pictures of the…was it "century"? No, that's too many movies. He said that Woody Allen wrote and directed it after his affair with Diane Keaton had fizzled out.

Now I'm not into movies much, but I had the impression that Hollywood people go in and out of relationships so often it doesn't hurt them as much as it does the rest of us. They can't let it. There are too many beautiful flakes out there to divert the pain and too many pressing ambitions that demand attention. It surprises me anyway that Diane Keaton could actually have fallen for Woody Allen; he is definitely not the typical movie star. This break-up was important enough to put down in black and white. I mean color.

So I run a bucket of soapy water and wring out the mop (your hands never touch the mop slop, they advertise), and I miss the beginning of the show. When I get back to the TV, the beautiful Diane Keaton (Annie Hall) is already attracted to Woody Allen (Alvie Singer). A likely story. But he was younger then and had almost a full head of hair, so maybe it's possible.

They're at a party. Annie Hall flirts, acts silly, and says dumb things to catch Alvie's attention, and he, getting her vibes, offers to take her home. "Oh, you have a car?" she asks coyly.

He says, "No, I thought I'd call a cab.

"I have a car," she says, and in an instant they're in a Volkswagen careening down the New York streets with a petrified Alvie urging her, in an understated way, to slow down, slow down. Straight off, we see Annie Hall's free spirit and Alvie's repressive nature.

Not earth shattering; not even mildly funny. I say, if it's a comedy, make me laugh. "MAKE ME LAUGH," I shout. I could just hear my Faith scream back: "Chill out, Ma!"

I never talked that way to *my* mother. Well, she immigrated from Japan, and I wouldn't have known how to say "chill out" in Japanese. Besides, that particular phrase hadn't yet been coined. And also I've not been the best Nisei mother. Nisei women are supermoms. Faith has probably wanted to throw a towel over my head many times. But she hasn't. Hey, she's not here; maybe she wouldn't have said that. I make things up as I go along; it's my other life.

Besides, the doors and windows are closed, I'm alone, and I can say anything I want, as loudly as I want. She's not here. No one is. Heck, I can belch over a can of soda; I can pass a couple of social no-no's, just like guys. Who sees? Who hears? WHO CARES?

That's why I'm alone now. That's why he left me. Well, no; I wasn't like that when he was around. That's not why he left me. See? If you live long enough, you even answer yourself.

I finish mopping, throw out the water, and set the mop outside. When I get back, Annie Hall has moved in with Alvie Singer. Alvie is wary. He's been married twice before, and he's cautious. Alvie is a cautious neurotic stand-up comic. He's seriously sensitive to anti-Semitic remarks like: "Jew eat yet?" "Jew care for a smoke?" "What Jew say?"

I can relate to that. I'm averse to the word "Jap." Even when it refers to Jewish American Princesses. I don't even like it when Japanese say it. I've been hearing "Jap" since my first contact with white people—in kindergarten by very young children. And later by older people, men and women, schoolteachers, and senators too. Lots of politicians. One said, "Once a Jap, always a Jap. Put 'em in the badlands and throw away the key."

When I was a little girl, my mother told me that racism prevails in America. When shopgirls wouldn't wait on us, she would stamp her feet and handle the merchandise roughly. "They're being rude because we're Japanese," she'd say very loudly in Japanese. "Let them know we know, and we don't like it." She would touch everything in reach and fling the merchandise down contemptuously. Mess up the counter. Once she even put on a store hat and made ready to take off with it. Anything to get attention.

We couldn't just go to another store because there was only this one main street in our country town—only one Sears, one five-and-dime, only one JC Penney, one Mode O'Day. There was a seed and fertilizer building on the outskirts. We did have two shoe stores: Karl's and Kirby's. The clerks were nicer there. Hurray for competition.

Still, my mother worried that we (she had three of us then) would not be able to function in white society, and she sometimes (when there was money) took us to the Woolworth lunch counter so we could learn to order food (banana splits and sundaes usually) and eat in public with the proper utensils. We even went to the "Garden City Restaurant," where one of her students' dad (she taught Japanese once a week at the Buddhist temple) was the cook. The meal I remember is a hamburger patty with one long green scallion and a mound of rice. We had more interesting meals at home. My father did not participate in these outings. He had nothing to prove.

"GO BACK WHERE YOU CAME FROM!" That was used a lot. Well, we couldn't do it because we didn't have boat fare (thanks to the Great Depression), and also my mother had promised her sister in Japan she would return a rich woman. Her pride wouldn't let her go back poor. My aunt told me this many years later, many years after my mother died (still pining to return).

I don't know why I went to Japan—maybe to prove to my mom it wasn't totally impossible (as though she could somehow see it from that little plot in San Diego). Also, I wanted to know if Japan was all she said it was: beautiful, wonderful, cherry blossoms in the spring, petals riding the wind like snow. *Like snow.*

Maybe I was just going in her place. It was my first visit—not going "back," as I had been admonished many years before. I thought of her all the way over, always yearning but never realizing her dream. I suppose I would have pined for America if I were unable to get back. I suppose I would always have remembered the white primrose covering the desert floor in spring or the sun fading on the wall of our old house. Maybe I was just saying to her, "IT'S DOABLE, MA! AND I FLEW. I DIDN'T GO STEERAGE, MA!" Well, I didn't make a promise like she did to her sister.

Racism is endemic; it's infectious. It colors your decisions and how you live your life. As a kid, you fight back: "Yeah? I'd rather be a Jap (I said it) than poor white trash like you!" "Go back where I came from? I was *born* here. Same as you, you dumb Okie!" Yes, I said that too. The cruel sound of some words never fade.

Most of Alvie Singer's jokes center around his racial paranoia and low self-esteem laced with an obsession with death. People laugh with him because, I guess, everyone has felt the pain of being on the outside and the fear of death. It's the old saying: When it hurts too much, you laugh, or you will cry.

Annie Hall is different. She's young, and a gentile, and has little concept of diaspora or Holocaust. She has only a nodding acquaintance with bias (do you like *foie gras,* or do you hate liver? No, that's from another movie). She loves people, she loves to laugh. All this Alvie stuff is too dark for one who's always been on the "inside." You know, a non-Jew.

Alvie brings home books, and Annie gets the hint but resents his efforts to make her more intellectual, more feeling, more hurting. Like him. Alvie wears her down with his need to change her. His obsessions are big baggage.

I can connect with that. Sid tried to change me too, but not intellectually. Nisei boys don't really care for smart girls.

Sid was my brother's friend. During the war my brother had been shipped off to a separate camp, and that's where he met Sid. After Japan was defeated, after we were released from camp, we tried to pick up our lost lives. My father died from bleeding ulcers just days before camp closed. He didn't have to worry about resettlement. My mother thought we ought to go to San Diego with the last contingent of evacuees, so my mother, my sister and her son (her husband was serving in a labor battalion in Alabama), and I moved to San Diego with the last group leaving camp. My brother joined us later. I found work in a photo-finishing plant and tried to save money for art classes in LA; my brother worked with a fishing crew.

Sid was a live-in schoolboy for a white family in Westwood. That means he was working, washing dishes, vacuuming, pruning trees, mixing drinks at a house party, taking coats, and so on. He was trying to get through UCLA without his dad's help. His major was political science.

My brother and Sid were going to a wedding for a couple they knew in camp. My brother had offered to give me a ride to my girlfriend's house that same day, but he had to pick up Sid first.

So we were all in the front seat, me in the middle, very cozy, very close. Cars were narrow then. Sid slipped his left arm over the back of the seat as though trying to make room. Okay. Then I felt his fingers gently stroke my shoulder. My scalp froze, but I said nothing. What could I say? KEEP YOUR FINGERS TO YOURSELF? My brother would be alarmed. It might break up their friendship. Sid pressed his thigh against mine. Well, that was kind of nice.

Sid was a very funny guy, easy to like, but because I wasn't interested in starting a relationship, I didn't do the girl thing with him. Well, not too much. And he seemed to be comfortable with that. We laughed a lot. I could tell he liked me, but I'd always been suspicious of fresh guys (what does he want from me? Oh, no, not *that*). And I didn't have much respect for guys who would consort with people like me (Alvie says that). I think I was afraid I might snag a loser, and I wasn't ready for a winner.

Sid suggested we get together after the wedding, but my brother said no, he had to hurry back to San Diego. He had a tuna boat to catch. When we got to my girlfriend's, Sid asked for my phone number; I told him I was moving to Los Angeles soon. "Well then, I'll give you mine. Call me when you get here," he said. My brother scowled.

At the end of the month I moved in with my girlfriend in East Los Angeles, got a part-time job, and was busy trying to get into Art Center School. The GIs were monopolizing the day classes, so I settled for a couple of night courses. I didn't call Sid, but the next month he wrote a letter (sent care of my brother) saying he was disappointed that I hadn't called him and gave me his phone number again. I called and we met again.

And again. And again. I couldn't believe it: could anyone really find me so engaging? I let myself like him. It felt good. Weekends we walked a lot and ate at food stands in the neighborhood: burritos, tacos, hamburgers, hot dogs. We rested on park benches. We went to cheap movies on skid row (Tyrone Power in *Nightmare Alley*). My girlfriend didn't care for Sid, so it was hard for us to stay at the house. Sometimes he took a streetcar with me to my class and then went on to the house in Westwood. That's a lot of trolley transfers.

Sid had a thing about germs. Never mind all those we swallowed in dirty restaurants. We got around by trolley, and he was careful not to touch doorknobs and poles with his bare hands. I held his arm while he hooked his other elbow around the metal bar set up to steady lurching riders. So that's the way we traveled. Unless we got seats. Me, I'm a country kid and used to dirt and bacteria. I told him we must look a sight, two Nisei reeling together like conjoined twins. He said, "Don't worry about it; you're with me." He remembered that his mother's hands smelled of Clorox. I never smelled my mother's hands.

The floor is hard; I am uncomfortable. The movie is making me restless. I can do a small load of wash. At least the whites. Wash-wash, clean-clean. What happened to the girl who wasn't afraid of a little dirt and sweat? Relax and watch the show. *Can't.* It's a personality disorder; accept it. Just go ahead and start the washer and save the analysis for later. I know this story already. It's like my own except for ethnic and economic differences.

From the service porch the sound of the dialogue is unmistakable. There are problems in the Annie-Alvie alliance.

Annie is sitting on the bed smoking pot. Alvie asks why she is so compelled to smoke that stuff all the time. "It relaxes me," she says. Is this before or after coitus? Either way, it's not a good sign.

But that's exactly how it is: while people continue their annoying habits, they don't notice changes in the relationship—the shift in attitude. Of course, in a movie, it's much faster. I get back, and the turn is dramatic. The romance is gone; the bickering is intense.

I met a guy in my art class who liked to talk to me. "You like baseball?" Ben asked. No. "Like to dance?" No. "Well, how about dinner and a movie, or a hike in Yosemite, or a yak ride to Shangri La?" he asked.

"Sounds like fun, but I have a boyfriend; he might want to come along," I said. I realized then how weighty our dependence had become. Ben was Chinese and didn't seem to have the hang-ups that Japanese have. He liked to hear me laugh and enjoyed my language excesses. Sid would say, "Don't use 'love' for every condition. You can't *love* a thing. Or *hate* a thing. A thing's a thing." Or, when I threw a snit, "Your dad should have given you a good spanking." Or, when we were talking among friends,

"Shhh shhh, lower your voice." Or, when I apologized (just to end an argument), "We can't go on like this." Not to continue sounded good. Oh, to be free again.

It's only halfway through the movie. There's a good forty-five more minutes of plot. Now it's clear that Annie Hall must leave Alvie Singer. It can't continue like that. It's too depressing; too confining. Annie packs up her stuff, and Alvie lets her go.

Ben had begun to look good to me. He was into commercial art and was already planning an agency of his own. His large prosperous family backed him fully. They dressed well, ate well, and laughed heartily.

Sid's family wasn't like that. His mother was a cool cat: no envy, no anger, no hate. She was very cultured and a fastidious cook. The Clorox hands were before the war when she did housework for a rich white family. After the war, when our temples were reactivated, she joined the Buddhist Women's Auxiliary and became an important official. Though she was always gracious, I knew she disliked me. Well, "dislike" is too strong. Apathetic. Sid's father died disliking me.

I tried to make nice to them, but they saw right through me. I was too country, too raw. Their eldest son was a doctor (did his internship in camp), their daughter was a university graduate, Sid had a political future in mind (what a dreamer), and I was a gauche country girl. They were politely condescending; that's the only way I could put it. But I was young and didn't care, and it wasn't Sid's fault. I knew he loved me. I think that's what galled them.

Annie Hall, Annie Hall. Of course she leaves Alvie. She moves into a small apartment. She sees other men.

I decided to end my relationship with Sid. After all, it's not like we had an affair or anything. I think we weren't intimate (well, we were very intimate, but not sexually) because among Nisei sex was serious business, and commitment was generally forever. In those days.

It was a piece of cake. There was no need for the preparation, practicing words to soften the break. After class, about 9:30 one evening, I ducked into a telephone booth, called Sid, and told him I wanted to call it quits. He was surprised but seemed relieved. He said, "If that's what you want."

"We're no good for each other." I think that was from a movie.

Where else would I get such dialogue? Never had to use words like that before. Well, I'd practiced them; no use wasting them.

"You must be right," he said. He didn't seem angry. We said good-bye.

I was free! For a five-cent phone call (that's what it cost) and an old movie line, I had freed myself. I felt truly liberated. That weekend I went out to dinner and a movie with Ben. We had fun. He asked for another date. We went out about four times.

I tried; I think I did, but it was no good. I was always thinking of Sid. It was less than honest. Unfair to Ben. I told him I wanted to get together with Sid again, but I doubted that he'd take me back; he was so proud and stubborn. Ben blew his stack: "What *is* this? Are you playing musical chairs with me?" I had never seen him so angry.

"I have to get back with him or nothing. My heart is breaking," I said. Ben looked ready to cry. He hugged me so tightly I thought my ribs would break. That was another first for him. But he let me go.

"No hard feelings," he said. And we continued to be friends at school.

Sometimes I can stare directly at the TV, but, if my mind is elsewhere, I see and hear only the discourse in my head. Then, in an instant, a word or gesture will bring me back to the TV (like changing channels), but, of course, I'll already have missed a lot. Sometimes I can reconstruct what I've lost.

Maybe not; if this movie is autobiographical, then Woody Allen either has a powerful internal invisible girl-magnet, or he's delusional. Here he is in bed with yet another beautiful woman. But it doesn't look like an affair of great proportions. No panting, no open-mouth kissing, just talking about another one of Alvie's obsessions. The phone rings. It's three in the morning, and Annie's on the phone asking, "Are you with someone?"

"No," Alvie says, "It's the radio." Annie cries; she misses him so much; she wants to come back.

"WAIT, ANNIE," I shout, "HOLD OFF. YOU HAVE TO WAIT. I *know* about these things. You have to hurt and wallow in pain; you have to eat it, sleep it, excrete it, until you get sick of it, bored with it. *Then* you move *on*. You don't move back *in*.

I wish someone had told me that. Maybe I would be with a guy who might have made me happier. Or just as miserable. Me-me-me; it was always about me.

Though Sid didn't say it, I think he felt the awful void too. Maybe he cried in his room as I did—quietly (so my friend wouldn't hear)—or maybe without tears so that he would hurt less. I cried into the phone too. It cost another nickel to ask him to take me back, to tell him how bleak the days were without him. "I will come see you tomorrow," he said. The joy. The joy.

Next day, Sid took off from his studies, and we went to Griffith Park. I made a couple of sandwiches, and we found an isolated spot in the woods and picnicked. We hardly ate or spoke. He spread his coat over the dry eucalyptus leaves, and we made love.

I kept thinking someone was lurking behind the trees, and I was very nervous. "Let them watch," Sid said. He didn't care. Let them watch; I was with him again. It was like returning home. "We should always be together," he said. No more hunger. No more thirst.

The Korean War was heating up, and there was talk of conscription. Sid's parents thought he should marry someone to avoid the draft. I don't think they cared who I was. AVOID THE WAR AT ANY COST was the message. It was almost funny. I know now, they didn't want their son to experience the horrors of war—to kill another family's son or, worse, to be killed. I know, because it's the way Sid was brought up. It's why the family was sent to a separate camp. It's why my brother was there too.

Sid quit his job and took a leave from school. We were married in his brother's house by a Buddhist minister with just our families present. My sister had a new baby with a bad allergy, and she cried all through the ceremony. My brother was very quiet.

Annie Hall goes back to Alvie. It doesn't work. After a few more bouts with Alvie, she leaves again. She moves to California with a new lover. Annie, the optimist.

Now, it's Alvie's turn. In his understated way, he feels the pain. He follows her to Los Angeles and begs her to come back to him. "Marry me," he pleads. Annie cannot be persuaded. He returns to New York without her. If he appears unscarred, it's because he's used to enduring; he's a Jew. And life, for both, moves on.

All the couples we knew were having babies but us. Sid said he didn't want to bring up kids only to send them off to war. "Another one will break out soon. You'll see," he warned.

"He'll miss it. He won't be old enough," I said. "Or it *might* be girl."

"Girls suffer too. Didn't you learn *anything* from the camp experience? Wars are fought for power, territory, or resources. *We're* the ones that get caught in it. *We*, the unwashed masses."

"I want someone to love me unconditionally."

"You have someone."

But my needs were huge and grew with the years. More attention, more everything. More than Sid could handle. He had wants too. He had to prove himself, and that was also consuming. He tried all sorts of avenues; insurance served him better than most. With insurance he was serving his community too.

And I had my way. I had my baby. My Faith. And for a while I stayed off Sid's back. Sid got involved in community activity. It suited his needs; it also helped get clients. He made appointments in the evenings after the work day. When he opened his own office, he was away day and night.

To keep busy, I fell in with Faith's PTA but very soon was drowning in the bureaucracy. I should have expected that; I'm not a people person. I joined an art class again. My instructor looked at my work and asked, "Where's the soul in this?" *Soul?* What did he mean? "It's beyond what you see with your eyes," he said. "When you find it, you'll never paint like this again." He pointed to my canvas.

Sid and I did not drift apart in grace. We waged bitter war—for power, for territory. And then he left. Faith said, "Can you blame him?" She had grown up. She loved her dad but still stuck by me. He found someone else to love. Someone compliant, younger, and prettier.

Faith bought a new dress for Sid's wedding. I watched her get ready; I felt betrayed. I said, "So you're really going."

She said, "I'm not deserting you, Mom." Then, "He's only trying to be happy. I've come to believe the main thing in life is to be happy." You *know* she didn't get that from me.

I had to give up painting because the pictures got so dark; I couldn't find the light. Couldn't find the soul. One night I felt so god-awful, I woke Faith from deep sleep and said, "I don't think I can make it, Faith."

She knew exactly what I meant. She said, "You'll make it, Mom. You're strong."

And I did: hour by hour, day by day. I let it go. And I learned things that, being a hardhead (to the max), I couldn't have learned any other way. There's no chain of command above or below. I'm the top and the bottom. I have not yet found "soul," but it's been an interesting search. I've started a running dialogue with myself to hold on to perspective, to sanity. It's a useful habit: "You did it, girl, hip hip hurray!" Or, "Now live with that." Or, "Here's where you swallow a little pride and do an about-face." Or, "I hear you." I HEAR YOU, ALVIE!

Yes, I hear you, and, as they say, Alvie, I feel your pain (Annie Hall is out of my league; I can't keep up with her eternal cheer). But, as you very well know, Alvie, wounds heal (if they don't kill you).

Did years pass before the day you bump into Annie Hall on a New York sidewalk? She had come back but not to you. You exchange a few friendly words, walk together a short block, then say good-bye.

Good-bye, Annie Hall. She blithely hops a curb to cross the street. The credits roll.

Onna

My niece Sandy tells me that almost everyone she talks to about her problems quickly redirects the subject to him or herself. "Well," I say, "almost everyone has similar experiences, and we just want to pass on what we've learned from them."

"Oh, Auntie," she sighs.

"Well," I say, "if you don't want a response, you might try talking to your sock, or shoe, or yourself. That way, at least you can say, 'You-you-you! I don't want to hear about *you*. I just want your support.'"

"That's true," she says. Still she comes to me when she is troubled. Or has a great idea.

Sandy is the third child of five of my beloved younger sister, who was like my own daughter. So it follows that all five are like my grandchildren. But I don't take the liberties I do with my daughter or grandchildren. I don't judge or advise. Unless I'm sorely pushed.

Sandy is also the one who talks intimately with me—about her friends and boyfriends, about her feelings and what she learns from them. My daughter doesn't do that. Which I understand. I wouldn't have wanted to tell *my* mother everything either—to have watched the color in her eyes change as I talked. That is, if she had stood still long enough to listen.

I guess that's the trouble with parent and child relationships. You listen to your kids from infancy to adulthood and assume they're saying the same things they've said through the years and that if you caught every third word, it would be enough to get the gist of the story.

That's why I took to writing. It's sort of like talking to your shoe. Or yourself. These things don't judge; they give you full attention. They don't say, "Have I told you what happened to me?" They're not thinking of what they're going to say next. They're not waiting impatiently for you to be done. And they're very forgiving when you don't make sense.

At first I just dabbled in writing. I stuck a tentative toe in the pond to try it out. If it was too cold, I could always pull back, saying, "I don't really mean to swim." Well, I don't know how to swim, and I was afraid of drowning.

Then after my mother died, I started writing about things closer to my heart. I wrote about my mother, who never got over her longing to return to Japan; about my silent father, who I didn't get to know or love; about our lives as nomadic Japanese on tenant farms in a depressed economy. I wanted to tell those stories; I could not let our lives fade as quietly as their hearts did. I pretended to talk to myself. So what if no one wants to listen; I could set things straight in my own mind. I didn't care anymore if I drowned.

Sandy is brave. She doesn't worry about drowning. She knows how to swim. She has survival skills. They all do—all five of my sister's children. Well, in our own way, my daughter and I do too. We will not die, like my mother, longing for something so far out of reach. We dream closer to home.

My sweet sister didn't have survival skills. She died after two long years of illness, and this close-knit family dealt with grief each in his or her own particular way: the boy joined a Zen center; the oldest girl married just months before her mother died and returned to Hawai'i with her husband. Sandy flew to England with boyfriend Roger to meet his parents and went on a backpacking tour of Europe and Southeast Asia with him. The third daughter moved to Hawai'i like the first. The fourth girl, still in her early teens, stayed with her father, who very soon met and married a young white woman.

No, it's not fair to say they all scattered after my sister's death. They were young adults, and they had their own agendas.

Eventually all of them coupled with white people. I don't know why this happened. Maybe, as Sandy later explained, there just weren't a lot of Japanese American boys in Santa Barbara, and those there simply were not interested in her.

Gardena was a Japanese enclave in pre–World War II California. Many of us also returned after the war. We did. We lived two blocks away from my sister's family and when they moved, it was like they tore a piece of us away. But they had great plans to start a landscape and maintenance business in Santa Barbara, a mostly white middle-class town.

Sandy and her older sister were in second and third grades. The first day of school, they came home crying. They said they were called "Japs." "What are 'Japs'?" they asked. I can imagine my sister's heartache as she comforted her little girls. Did they decide then that it wasn't such a good thing to be "Japs"?

I personally like being Japanese. My mother told me to hold my head high. "Japanese are the best," she said. "We have a proud history." I also like Japanese men. The few movies I had seen as a child were flickering black-and-white samurai epics, and I loved the swordplay, the bravado, the male endurance and grit. I liked the scratching, hissing, and loping too.

Of course, American-born Japanese boys were not so bold (I think racism does that to people), but they did have a lot of endurance and grit. Look what they accomplished as American soldiers during World War II while we, their families, were incarcerated. In America. Who ever thought these innocent farm boys who'd never killed anything bigger than a chicken would take to shooting human beings? Or lay down their lives to fight for a freedom they never truly experienced. The 442nd was the most decorated (segregated) battalion in the American army during World War II.

And there were the camp "resisters" who wouldn't report to the induction center until the government let our people go. They spent two years in prison for this moral stand, and time proved them as least as courageous as the soldiers who went to war.

These are the men of my generation. You rarely heard them cry or complain or brag, even as old men. They smiled while their hearts were broken and tried to make light of everything. My mother would say that's part of the heritage, part of our "proud history"—the endurance, the patriotism (whatever the nation), the grit.

I identified with Japanese women, too. They, like me, had straight black hair and almond eyes. And I, like them, had been brought up as *onna*, a woman; *makete katsu* was a big part of our identity as women. That means to win by losing. With grace. That's the hard part. But, in spite of my mother's effort, I can't say I was always successful in either department. My little sister was a natural. She was gentle and forgiving and didn't mind giving in.

Sandy doesn't understand this concept. She says, "But Auntie, you have to speak up for your feelings. Otherwise, what do you do with them? You can't let them rankle in your belly not ever finding peace."

Well, you can. I do. Let me correct that: I did for many years. Not so much now. When you grow older, some of the old energy leaves, and you don't care that much what you say. Nobody listens anyway. But I have kept stuff rattling around for a long time. I was so indoctrinated I often didn't recognize anger until much later, when it bubbled up in an indigestible glob and I thought, "I could have said, 'Blah-blah' or 'Bleh-bleh' instead of working up that awful grin." The bad part: sometimes it came out anyway— in a wave of anger without victory, without grace. The joy stayed underground too.

Sandy is liberated; she is direct and honest. Still she has those gentle and giving qualities of *onna* like her mother. Maybe it's the ancestral genes. But she stands her ground; she does not win by losing; she maintains her position and grace. It's a neat trick if you can pull it off.

Her siblings say, "Sandy likes to talk. She explains everything and won't let go"; and after considerable argument (they don't easily give in either), they do the *makete katsu* and walk away with their eyes glazing over. But it's more than just talking. There's stuff that Sandy has to get *out*.

Among her early boyfriends was Roger. She met him while attending college and working in a five-star hotel waiting tables. She was studying interior decorating; he was bartending there. He was from England.

My sister worried that Roger was prone to spinning tall tales, unbelievable stories of his "adventures." "He talks too much," she said.

"Well, he's a bartender," I said. "That's his job."

"I know," my sister said.

"Sandy can take care of herself, and if she hasn't found him out, she soon will. Or maybe it doesn't matter to her," I said.

"That's what I'm afraid of," my sister said.

Then, on leap day of 1984, my little sister died. And Sandy and Roger flew to England to meet his parents. Maybe she was looking for another mother. She wrote letters about the trip. It was as though she were keeping a record of her growth and changes. She was twenty-two.

They first visited Roger's parents in England and bought a van there. They toured parts of Europe in the van, which they planned to sell in Athens before continuing through Turkey, Cairo, and India (where it's warm, she said) on trains, planes, or what have you, but they couldn't find a buyer for the car, so they decided to return to England to either sell it or leave it with Roger's folks.

Thinking Sandy would be lonely for home, my daughter and I had sent a slew of letters in care of Roger's parents, and Sandy was so happy to hear from us she started writing these letters.

On their trip back to England, they were on the top of the Italian boot, and they had 1,500 miles to do in two and a half days. From Geneva, Switzerland, they headed for Dijon, France, on a bald rear tire, without chains, in dead winter, in the Alps.

It was cold and snowing. They were told to forget the shortcut. "The road will be frozen over," the old-timers warned. But they were young and vigorous and too smart for old waggling heads. They took the shortcut.

Soon it was too late to turn back. Roger would climb a few feet up the mountain and slide back double the gain. Up the frozen road and slithering down, up and down, they were hours on the icy pass. Sandy was sure they would die there, the gas running out, the van tumbling over the mountainside. They would be found, maybe the next day, or in spring, or a century later, clinging together, frozen in prayer. Finally Roger asked Sandy to get out and walk alongside the van; if it should go down, he said, there was no sense in two of them getting killed.

Sandy said no, they would live through this or die together. It was as though, from the day they were born, through Roger's incredible and harrowing adventures through England, Canada, and on the coast of California and Sandy's tentative forays in search of herself, their lives had moved inexorably toward each other and these final hours on that frozen mountain pass.

Then Roger got the idea that if Sandy, the baggage, and everything movable were piled in the rear of the van, maybe the weight would give the tires some traction. Slowly they moved forward. Sandy cheered for all the souvlakis and baklavas she'd enjoyed in Greece. Like another answer to their prayers, a heavy truck appeared before them and churned up the road so they could make it safely to the main highway. It took them five hours to drive 105 miles; two hours for the first 12 miles.

After leaving England the second time, they backpacked their way through Cairo and India, fought off the hopeless beggars ("Oh, Auntie, it would break your heart," she wrote), stepped over their feces, occasionally stayed in a cheap hotel, sprayed everything with Lysol, made love on gray sheets (I suppose).

In a small village in Burma, Sandy caught a bug and grew very sick with a high fever and vomiting. Now without a car, they had to take an open cart to get to a modern doctor in the next city.

The townspeople were celebrating an ancient festival; part of the ritual was dousing travelers and passersby with water. Villagers lined the country road gleefully throwing buckets of water at the cart. Roger stood by Sandy, shielding her from the water, wringing out the blanket that covered her, and screaming to the villagers, "She's sick! Don't you see, she's sick?" The villagers shrieked back with joy, happy for the foreigner's vigorous response to their festivities. They lived through that too.

Sandy said she was learning a lot about herself. She realized now that she was rushing through her life, not savoring the important things. She said she was not going to stress over small things any more. She said, "I'm not sure what I'll do when I get back, but I'm not going to think about that now."

I didn't know then that what she didn't want to think about was the state of her relationship with Roger. They returned from their trip flat broke, an 18,000-dollar odyssey.

Sandy and Roger spent their last $350 in Tokyo, borrowed money from her married sister in Hawaiʻi, and limped home to Santa Barbara. And they broke up.

"I don't get it," I said. "I thought the whole idea of the trip was to tack down the relationship. To meet the parents; to test the connection." It wasn't something I would have endorsed had I been consulted. Only rich white women did that—traipse all over Europe with a man and then decide a permanent alliance wouldn't work. What happened? "Don't you get closer when you go through so much together?" I asked. "Didn't Roger prove his love for you?"

"It isn't Roger. It's me. I still have some exploring to do," Sandy said. She didn't mean traveling. She said she didn't know who she was. She had to find out.

"Those things take time," I said. "Old as I am, I don't know who I am either." And I may never find out. And who cares?

"I can't live like that," she said. "I need to know more about myself, and I can't do it staying with Roger." She said Roger was way ahead of her. He already knew who he was. That's what he claimed, I guess.

My sister's observations of Roger's tall tales came to mind. I didn't know Roger well. The only stories I heard directly from his lips were ghost stories.

It was the year before my sister died. Sandy and Roger had dropped by on their way to Disneyland. There were the three of us, and, for some reason, probably casting about for something to share, we started talking about ghosts.

Roger said in his youth in England, he was a door-to-door salesman. He sold encyclopedias. The salesmen went in pairs in company cars to remote villages, a mission to bring encyclopedic knowledge to villagers bogged in centuries of misinformation. Well, they did have the telly. Get them past the intellectual desert, you might say.

One day they were in this very old town; the weather turned bad and nobody was buying, so Roger and his mate ducked into a roadside booth to report to the company. While Roger was on the phone, he noticed his partner turning pale, his eyes bulging. Roger turned and saw the ghost. "How do you know it was a ghost?" I asked.

He said, "At first I didn't, you see. Thought the bloke was waiting to get on the phone. Well, it was pouring rain, and this man had no umbrella, no slicker, no rubbers, and he wasn't wet. Besides, his clothes were like seventeenth-, eighteenth-century peasant, you know?"

Well, they bolted. Left the sample books in the booth and took off. They ran for about a hundred yards or so, and, winded (too many cigarettes, I suppose), they stopped and looked back. The ghost had silently followed, still dry, still staring at them. By luck, they found the car and, in the driving rain, sped back to the shop.

Barring some embellishment, I had no doubt Roger was telling the truth. There were other stories: he said there was a hospital in London that was reputed to be haunted. After a remodeling, the ghosts continued to appear but only the upper half, since the lower part still walked the floor that was demolished. If Roger was teasing, it was quite a creative joke.

He was at the funeral, but I don't remember talking to him. My sister's brother-in-law, pastor of a small Baptist church, had asked me to say a few words to the congregation, but I couldn't talk. This was my little sister's funeral, a gentler, more giving, more forgiving person than I. And she had gone on before me. I couldn't speak to anyone, so I don't suppose I talked to Roger. In fact I'm not sure if he was actually there, and, if I saw him again, I don't think I'd recognize him.

Learning about people is like peeling an onion. The first layers may sting the eyes a bit, but, until you pare them away, you can't get to the core. That is, if you care to take the trouble. Sometimes the core is the same as the surface; that's not all bad. That's probably what Sandy meant when she said Roger already knew who he was and he accepted that. Maybe the Roger of those incredible stories was sitting there at the heart of the Roger we knew all the time; that was the real Roger from inside to out, and maybe it wasn't enough for Sandy. Or maybe she found a fake Roger.

Well no, I don't think that. I believe Roger; I think he's a sincere person. Crazy things were always happening to him. Roger is a man who likes to put himself at risk. He pushes himself to the edge, unafraid to bottom out, exhilarated by the crash and upward climb. The old adrenaline rush. That's why he was always getting in and out of trouble.

Also, I know couples who got along better in hard times and times of stress when they were pulling together with total passion. And when good times rolled in, they were unable to stay together. Some couples fall apart when success visits the twosome. Their needs changed.

But that wasn't the case here. For the first time in Roger's rough-and-tumble life, he had experienced such giving. He didn't want to leave Sandy. He loved her. And she loved him too, she said. They both cried when they said good-bye. They were in a parking lot, and she drove away alone in the rain. A real movie scenario.

Some of us are born tragedians. Maybe it's in our family genes. It was years before I learned it wasn't necessary to flog myself so relentlessly. After all, we're only here for a short time, and why not just dance lightly on the surface? Nobody cared and nobody was watching.

Roger left town. It was too painful to be near Sandy; and he didn't want that kind of pain. He was man enough for anything else. He moved to Hollywood, found a job in the movie business, and later married a young Latina who needed a green card and went on to have children with her.

I could tell that was hard on Sandy, but that was her choice. Divorce hadn't been my choice, but when I stopped thinking of my ex every minute of every day, I was ready to move on. Actually, after he remarried, I knew he wasn't thinking about me; so I let him go, along with most of my anger. So when Sandy stopped talking about Roger, I knew she would be all right. For sure, he was all right. He had his hands full.

A few years later, Sandy met Vince, who was also from Europe—Switzerland. Vince was handsome; they made a lovely couple. He worked as a pastry chef in the same hotel. He was perfect, Sandy said. They were so compatible, so close, there wasn't anything, any problem they couldn't work out, she said.

This didn't mean that she knew herself any better but that with Vince there was the romance and excitement of exploring together. I think. She dropped out of college. It was a beautiful wedding with attendants, ushers, gowns and tuxedos, soulful vows, and a lovely champagne reception. There was nothing to mar this cloudless merger. They even bought a house.

But Vince brought along baggage Sandy hadn't understood. Maybe he hid it from her, or maybe she knew and thought it could be ironed out. I know plenty about baggage; it's tenacious. You can lock it in a closet, but it always sneaks out when you're not watching the door. Sometimes you think you've lost it for good, but it shows up in another form at another place.

I learned later that Vince was a child of a long-term affair between a wealthy tycoon and his beautiful mistress. Her beauty bought her a life as a piece of a man's agenda, a constant weighing of priorities and sacrifices. There was no place in this relationship for a baby, and Vince was shunted off to a childless couple in a small village nearby. I suspect his rich father paid the boy's board and care, but here also was an absence of love and intimacy. There was an understanding that it was not an adoption, so maybe the couple resisted a deeper attachment. His mother, beautifully groomed, made sporadic visits with extravagant gifts, but his father was always busy. Or didn't feel well. Or had a meeting. When Vince was old enough, he was sent to a boarding school and then to a military academy.

I suppose there were lots of kids of that economic strata abandoned in boarding schools or moved from school to school, but Vince was a loner and found no comfort in these comrades in misery. As soon as he was old enough, he left the academy to find his own way. He went to Paris, took a course in culinary arts, and became a chef specializing in pastry. Food of love.

Just from looking at Vince, dignified, self-assured, you would not have believed what rattled in his heart. Problems began to surface soon after the marriage. Small things, strange things. Once Sandy took Vince's wallet to pay for something, and, when she put the change back, he went ballistic. The bills should have been returned to his wallet in order of value with all the presidents facing the same way.

"Pretty childish, isn't it?" Sandy asked.

I made like one of those dream analysts. Maybe Sandy entering Vince's life was disturbing the order and philosophy he'd laid out through the loveless childhood years—a way of avoiding disappointment and pain by fixing a proper value and place for each relationship and gauging the emotional investment. Oh boy.

"Well, if that's true," Sandy said, "then it's not really his fault. He can't help it. He'll just have to learn to trust me." It sounded simple enough.

And she tried. I know Sandy well enough to know that. She's fair and kind. She's nurturing, and she would have done a lot of that with Vince. She's strong. If she can't fix it or make it better, she lets it go. I knew that when she broke up with Roger. It was something she couldn't make well until she first worked on herself.

So I fought my Japanese inclinations and left her alone. The Japanese seem to think it takes a village to negotiate a marriage; there are go-betweens called *baishakunin* who check family history and orchestrate meetings—the arranged marriage. And the Japanese think it takes a community to keep a marriage functioning. Actually it takes a gargantuan effort from the wife.

It did not go well. Vince and Sandy decided to move to Florida to start a new life without the problems they had in Santa Barbara. Vince applied for and got a job as chef in another fancy hotel. They planned to drive to Florida early and make a leisurely tour of the southern states. Sandy looked forward to it.

In the middle of Arizona (the first leg of the journey), something happened that Sandy would not divulge. I suppose it was another silly problem like the money in the wallet, with the resulting hysterics. Sandy asked to be taken to the airport.

It was amazing. In mid-sentence, Vince made an about-face. Without apology, without acknowledging what had transpired just seconds before, he spoke cheerfully about the next town. Sandy was so boggled, she didn't remember what town. "We'll find a sidewalk café," he said. "Outdoors would be nice, don't you agree? Just breathe the crisp Arizona air. What would you like to eat?" Food for love.

Sandy knew this was his form of apology, but she stood her ground and took a plane home. She cried for a month, every day, all day. It was probably no easier for Vince. After the worst crying was over, reality set in. Now she had to find a job.

One day the phone rang, and Sandy was offered a position managing a small restaurant in town. She put away her grief and went to work. The job was all hers. She hired and fired and set policy. She worked on the menu, cooked and washed dishes in a pinch, redecorated, rearranged the kitchen, redesigned the uniforms, took on an assistant, and shared her bonus with the kitchen staff. There wasn't time left to cry over Vince. And she didn't want to. She was happy, and the restaurant prospered.

"Auntie," she said, "you just have to have faith. Things will happen when they're supposed to." As though I didn't know, as though I hadn't relied on that most of my life. At least when I got a little wiser. I could have told her, but would she have heard me?

Vince and Sandy talked almost weekly, but now the situation was different. Sandy said that she still loved him and probably always would, but it wasn't a plea to get him back. It wasn't an apology. She said that he may one day want to return, but she was going on with her life and would not be waiting for him. She thought he should do the same. And maybe get some counseling. "It really helps," she said.

So they were amicably divorced. Since property values had fallen, there was no equity in the house, and Vince gave up his claim on it. There was little else to divide; the vintage car belonged to Vince.

A few years later, after he'd fulfilled his contract, Vince returned to Santa Barbara. His rich father had died and didn't leave him so much as a handkerchief to drop a tear on. His mother, I suppose, went on to another rich man.

Vince came back to Sandy. But it was too late. She had gone on with her life and found another love. But she let Vince stay at the house until he got on his feet, which meant finding an apartment and a job and once again giving up the ghost of their marriage.

Bill worked in a branch office of a national delivery service across the street from Sandy's workplace. He often had lunch there. Sandy said, "Can you imagine? He offered to buy me a drink at my bar. Well, I didn't want the whole kitchen staff watching us, so I suggested we go out. That was our first date."

At first, I didn't really like Bill. He was too tall. I didn't see how Sandy could like a fellow so tall that, with both of you standing, he could only see the top of your head. Not fat but big: big hands, big feet, big smile, huge gestures. Bill came on like a tidal wave.

By comparison, my ex was small. I could look him in the eyes without standing on my toes. But his scope was large. He got his degree in political science; he had hoped to help in the reconstruction of Japan, but we met and fell in love and married, and, while we were paying the mortgage and utilities and bringing up our daughter, Japan surged ahead and raised itself from the ashes without him. He was proud. It proved Japan's resilience and stamina. He was also resilient. He loved Japanese products: the TVs, stereos, and cameras, and we bought a lot of them. In that respect, we participated in Japan's rebirth.

My ex's heart was big. In the early postwar years, when we were released from the camps and permitted to return to California, there were thousands of us casting about for jobs and housing. He worked in a Japanese American employment agency hoping to be helpful to the returning evacuees. It hurt him to place so many bright young people in menial jobs—houseboys, maids, factory hands. It hurt him to see them work so efficiently and cheerfully. He brought some of them home.

I didn't like being housemother to his new friends. I was too needy myself. He said there was not enough attention in the world to satisfy my needs. He was right. I fought twenty-five years for my share of his love.

Then he left me. I should have waited quietly like a good Japanese wife, but I didn't, and he found a real Japanese woman. She was young and pretty. He married her, had two sons, and died during the Rodney King race riot. Burning and looting were happening all over, not just in Watts this time. My ex had called to ask if we were safe and died a few days later of asthma while being treated for cancer. The last time I saw him alive was at the hospital. The tumor in his brain had been removed, and his head was bandaged. His wife and youngest son were visiting too. The boy asked him, "What are you giving me for my birthday?"

My ex glanced quickly at me before he answered, "Nothing."

Once I told a friend that I would have done anything to hold my marriage together, and she said, "But you didn't."

"How can you say that?" I asked indignantly.

"Well, he's not with you now, is he?" she said. "So you didn't do *everything*."

"I did as much as I could, given the person I am," I amended. "How's that?"

"Better," my friend said.

Sandy brought Bill to our family holidays. He did not hang around Sandy's dad or her stepmom, who is white like himself. This branch of the family was rapidly turning lighter. Instead Bill seemed eager to make contact with me.

He tried to converse in Japanese. He asked me questions about *kanji* (Japanese written words) and the literal meaning of some phrases. I couldn't always help him. Sometimes he followed me while I carried platters from stove to table.

I felt uncomfortable with him. "He's trying too hard," I told my daughter. "I think he's a Japanophile."

"Then he's barking up the wrong tree; Sandy isn't really Japanese," my daughter said.

"That's right," I said. "And neither are you."

"And neither are you," she remarked.

My mother would have agreed, but that wasn't altogether true. I tried hard to remember all those rules she laid down for me from early on: a proper

Japanese girl does not sit like that. She obeys, does well in school, dresses modestly, keeps her legs together, is pleasant, everyone likes a pleasant smile. She kept these coming throughout her work in the kitchen, at the sewing machine, at the washboard, and on the farm. Well, they weren't presented in long formal lectures. Bits were hurled over her shoulder, hissed between clenched teeth, exhorted over furrows of seedlings as I walked home from the rural school. "Change your clothes; wash the rice!" I can hear her now.

But if she was bitter, it didn't always show. She was an *onna*. She was one of four daughters of a merchant's second marriage. Her father's business was packaging tea, and he always retained a working crew. Her mother, a sharp woman for her time, became his secretary and receptionist. They kept a cook, a maid, and various *amah*, wet nurses for the babies. My grandfather was a big man in the village. His girls were not accustomed to menial labor.

I asked my mother, then how was it that she married an impoverished immigrant farmer in America; didn't she have a shot at one of the classier village boys?

"Your father wasn't always poor," she snapped. "It's a depressed economy now."

It was a long story. My grandfather's first wife bore him a baby girl, which was not acceptable; the man had his heart set on a son. Now, of course, we know it wasn't her fault, but, in those days in Japan, a husband's decision was law, so the first wife was banished with that first mistake. There was no "three strikes and you're out" here. The old man made all the rules. The baby girl stayed with him.

I suppose there were other reasons for the banishment, because my grandfather then married my grandmother, a woman who bore him three consecutive daughters. But he didn't divorce her. My mother was the middle daughter.

In a Japanese family without sons, a process called *yoshi* is frequently practiced. A groom, usually from a family of many sons, is found for one of the daughters. He takes on her family name and business.

When the daughter of my grandfather's first wife was ready to marry, the *baishakunin* gleaned the ranks and found a proper *yoshi* for her. The *yoshi* was bright and hard-working. The business thrived. But later my grandmother unexpectedly became pregnant again (she was probably a very young bride), and this time she gave grandfather a baby boy. There was a great celebration.

Now the *yoshi* felt very threatened. The business he had worked so hard to build would be handed down to the son. His status in the family and the village would fall and his budding family humiliated.

The *yoshi* started embezzling, putting away money for himself in a hidden account, and before long the company went bankrupt. It was a terrible disgrace. The *yoshi* was not taken to court but was stripped of the family name and banished from the village. The *yoshi's* wife was given the choice of whether to stay with the family or go with the husband.

She chose to leave with him. Of course. She didn't owe loyalty to a father who had cast out her mother just because she was not the son he'd hoped for. With such a history, what would happen to her own children? They left as a family, and no one heard of them again.

"Now that's a real *onna*," I said. She stood up for her feelings, her children, and her man. My mother glared at me.

The family was bankrupt and disgraced, and, without a dowry, marriage prospects for my mother were not good. Maybe the only man available was my father, who was the first son of a Shimizu *kamaboko-ya*, a fish-cake maker. A young adventurer, my father had gone to America to pick the gold off the streets. He had worked in a dairy, a laundry, and as a farmhand; he was a good son and had often sent money and gifts to his family in Japan. He had returned in modest prosperity to find a bride. He planned to go back to America and start a farm of his own (he didn't know about the Alien Land Law). He was tall for a Japanese and lean, not very handsome, and no young buck, but he was responsible and strong, and I suppose he had a certain appeal. He would not have been my choice, but my mother did not reject him.

My mother was a lovely nineteen, and I'm sure my father could not believe his luck. He was twelve years older.

After the wedding, they set sail for America. She promised her sisters she would return in great wealth and pull the family up on its collective feet. These were the last spoken words she had with her sisters.

The tenant farming in America did not go well, and my mother did a lot of nagging: why didn't he plant tomatoes (like she said) instead of summer squash, which this year wasn't worth the cost of harvesting? Or vice versa.

My father didn't argue; he just walked away. He didn't show his emotions, good or bad. He rarely praised his children or uttered tender words to his wife. Maybe he was nicer before the hard times, before I came on the scene. Or maybe that was Japanese machismo. Sometimes he teased my mother. Once I heard him ask her why she sighed so deeply.

He loved her more than I knew. When money jangled in his pockets, which was not often, he bought her gifts: a ladies' wristwatch, a fancy bathrobe, a faux fur jacket, presents for a lady, not things she could use on a dusty desert farm. He himself wore khaki work pants and chambray shirts in the fields and to town. My mother complained about that too, but she didn't change him. She never returned to Japan with wealth or without it. If she was bitter, I could not blame her.

So my grandmother's unexpected son and my step-uncle's devious betrayal led to my mother's marriage to my father, and I was born a Japanese in America. Otherwise I would have been a proper Japanese daughter of a wealthy merchant, and my mother would have been happier. But I don't know that.

Later, much later, after the war, after I met and married my husband, when my mother lay in bed sicker than I realized, I said, "Mom, I wish I could have sent you to Japan. Once. Just once."

"No," she said, "this is the way it was to be."

"You worked so hard for so long and had so little reward," I said.

"Those were the best years," she said. "This is my reward."

Maybe she was talking about my father's silent adulation. He had passed on nine years earlier, just days before we left camp. Maybe she made her peace with the person I am. I had always thought I was a deep disappointment, but maybe she finally brought her sights down and accepted our karma. Maybe she was talking about my little sister.

Whatever my failings, I did try to pass along some of my mother's rules to my daughter: the superficial ones—wear your sweater, wipe that pout off your face—and some things a little below the surface—reach down and try to find a little compassion. My daughter did her best, but her very nature, like mine, was not to comply. But she was easier, nicer. "Yes, yes," she'd say, and, "I'm sorry." With that, she'd close the door.

I should have told her straight from the top, "To thine own self be true," but I didn't. I didn't know there was such a choice. I thought we were just rebellious, obstinate. But she turned out okay. I still have her love; or she's grown to love me; or she feels pity for me. Whatever, I'm lucky.

At first I dismissed Bill; after all, I didn't have to like everyone Sandy brought us. But sometimes people inadvertently reveal themselves in short bits, here and there, now and then, and when you piece it all together, a fuller picture emerges.

One day, Bill told me this little bit of a story: he was backing out of a parking space just as a young black kid was passing the passenger side door. Out of habit, Bill reached over to punch down the lock. He saw the kid's eyes roll, saw the sigh of resignation. Bill said, "Once in a while, his face comes back to me. He was only a kid, and I made him feel like that."

Sandy and her assistant left their old jobs and started a restaurant of their own. They had big plans: they would rent the space next door, convert it to a bakery, bake great loaves of bread and delectable pastries, and feature them at the restaurant. "The menu will be eclectic and changing," she said, "Cajun, French, Italian, Greek, Armenian—it'll be wonderful! No English, no hamburgers, no hot dogs."

"No Japanese?" I asked.

"Well, maybe. But no sushi," she said. "It's so exciting. There's so much to do. Got to find a good kitchen crew, waiters, bus people, a hostess.... I'll do that myself for a while. We have a chef lined up."

"Well, you have a loyal staff at your old place. Why don't you take them with you?" I asked. But she wouldn't do that to her boss.

"Why not?" I asked. "He wasn't very fair with you. He broke most of his promises."

"I know," she said. "But I don't want to take revenge. I don't like that. Anyway, by the law of averages, his errors will catch up with him." Vince offered his expertise, but she told him she already had a chef. Besides, she wanted to do this all by herself with, of course, her partner. She spent a lot of time with him. Away from Bill.

"How does he feel about that?" I asked. "How does he feel about Vince?"

"Oh, he doesn't mind," she said. "That's what's really great about

Bill. He trusts me totally." Apparently. He also didn't mind that Vince lived in the house, shared the bathroom, and cooked great meals for Sandy, who had not eaten at home for a long time.

"You mean Bill doesn't care? What's the matter with him?" I asked.

"He's a great guy," Sandy said. "He'd be hard to duplicate."

He was both. One month, he flew to Tennessee twice. I thought they were business trips, but Sandy said Bill's younger sister was in fragile emotional health and Bill went to keep her company. She was married and had children, but only Bill could comfort her. She only trusted Bill.

Bill's parents were divorced when he was four and his sister was just a toddler. His mother put them in day care and went to work. They relied heavily on each other for support and love. When Bill was eleven, his mother said she was through with caring for children and sent them to his father, who had married a woman who brought along two sons from a previous marriage. She was very partial to her own boys and gave Bill and his sister an awful time. They comforted each other and wept together; his sister grew to never trust anyone but Bill. They stayed in their father's house until Bill was old enough to work, then his sister married. She was not always happy. Her depression decimated her; she knew, just knew, one day her husband would desert her just like everyone else. But she knew Bill would always be there for her. And he was.

I loved my little sister too. I think I should tell the whole story here.

My mother, like her own mother, had two sets of children. In the span of three years my older sister, my brother, and I were born. As the eldest sibling, my sister made a lot of sacrifices and had many responsibilities. My brother, as soon as he was able, was manning the plow and guiding the horse. On icy winter mornings he helped my father light bonfires in the fields to keep the young plants from freezing. Still a boy, he was awakened at ungodly hours to bundle up and wordlessly trudge to the fields behind my father. I was glad not to have been born a boy.

In spite of my siblings' many chores, they still found time to gang up on me and tease and harass me. I was often in a state of agitation. My mother said that I should mind my elders. Seniority is the name of the game among Japanese.

When I was twelve, my mother gave birth to a baby boy. She was not so crazy about starting a new family—the crying, the nursing, the diapering, the incredible exhaustion again—but my sister and I were delighted. We fought for the baby's attention. At last I would have a friend. This little guy would be on *my* team. I played with him before I went to school and could hardly wait to come back to him.

When the baby was five months old (to the day), he drowned in a shallow tub of water not more than a few inches deep. My mother wailed, "I killed him! I left him only a minute. I killed him!"

I was heartbroken. I didn't think I would ever be the same again. All day long, the picture of him trying to lift his head, gasping for air, water rushing into his lungs, haunted me. At night he came to me, still breathing, laughing, his skin warm to the touch.

Though the word was frightening and never mentioned, my mother was suicidal. For once we rallied together in her support. We were underfoot all the time to remind her that we were there, dependent; she could not die. In desperation, she consulted a psychic in Los Angeles, and he advised her to have another baby. "Your son is trying to find the way to leave. Your unceasing grief is blocking his soul's path. Start living again. A new baby waits to join you," he said.

So my little sister came to us already burdened with enormous tasks. She did her job and left us, never knowing our gratitude. I never told her this story. Now that she's gone, there hardly seems any purpose in telling it, except that if you leave out any part of your journey from here to there, something's not going to make sense. Sandy knows that.

Sandy's in good hands. The really big thing about Bill is his ability to forgive. He has forgiven his parents, his stepmother, and his stepbrothers. He found this was the best way to deal with the bouts of depression that sometimes threaten to overwhelm him. He taught himself to let the past go and allow the condition to pass. And it always did. He has also forgiven me.

After a few years together, talk of a wedding surfaced. Sandy and Bill planned a ceremony in Peru in the Andes. Close to the clouds. Close to the natural spirits of the earth.

Then Sandy called to say it was all off. Bill had left her. The words she chose were "He dumped me."

"It's all right, Auntie," she said. "I wanted commitment; I wanted children, and he couldn't handle it."

I thought of Bill's observations of marriage and his stepmother's cruelty; his sister's bottomless melancholy may have scared him off. But I kept my mouth shut. Who needs talk at this point? Bill would be in a deep funk. I nearly cried.

"It's all right," Sandy said. "There's always my work."

"And there's always *you*," I said. "You're getting closer to finding it, aren't you—the you that you were looking for?" I wouldn't have gone to Peru anyway.

"Well," she said, "I don't know. I don't know if I know any more than I did then. I think love is everything. It's happiness. It's sharing your triumphs and sorrows. I still love Bill, and I think he loves me. He's still a good man. He'll work this out; he just sort of panicked."

I have a friend who said of her husband, "I know him. He'll do the right thing." She meant he'll eventually straighten out and return to her. He didn't.

I too thought my husband would come back, that he would remember the years we shared when hormones were raging and love and tenderness were unexplored territory, new and exploding with discoveries. I thought he wouldn't forget the way we were always there for each other.

He only remembered the things I should have done but didn't, the things I should not have done but did. He started a brand new life with a pretty young wife. Of course, they each brought along their own personal baggage to feather their nest. I could have told him that, but that's another thing he didn't like about me—too free with advice. Now his Japanese wife would just keep her thoughts to herself and win by losing. The old *makete katsu* ploy.

Unlike my friend's husband, unlike mine, Bill came back to Sandy. They do that, Sandy's men. They leave, taste freedom, find loneliness, and they come back.

Vince was long gone when Bill moved in with Sandy again—I guess to sort of ease into the commitment mode. They seemed more set-tled, happier.

This time they plan to marry in Tibet. Sandy is so busy with the restaurant and all, she no longer calls to give me the lowdown, and I don't do e-mail or fax. I suppose too there's plenty of work preparing for the trip: announcements, travel and hotel reservations, instructions to leave for the restaurant. No entourage this time. No bridesmaids or ushers. No tuxedos or gowns.

They'll need warm clothes. I don't know what it is with Sandy and high, cold places. I prefer flatlands. I like the plains. I like the dry heat, the bitter landscape. I like the still sorrow of emptiness. I was born to it.

A Christmas Orange Story

This is the fourth Thanksgiving we've spent with Jay and Penny in Oak View, a village near Ojai, California. They have a long house that sits on the broad spine of a hill, and their back porch looks out to the mountains beyond and the highway that dips in and out, stringing little clusters of buildings together. From there they can watch the big summer sky slowly darken from east to west, watch the darting headlights of cars speeding home on the ribbon of dust that hangs over the road.

The complex looks like an old homestead. There are two horse stalls, a pigpen, and a chicken coop. All the animals are long gone; the stands are now only crumbling wood and rusted wire. Dry needles and leaves of ancient pines and elms cushion the ground. There is a sump that sometimes emits pungent odors. Buzzards spin overhead.

On these Thanksgiving evenings on the porch, I feel a quiet amazement at all that transpired before, all that changes and continues to change. It seems important to set it down before, like the orange sunset, it disappears altogether: the bucolic setting where we feel the silent movement of time, the creeping knowledge that we, like the horses, pigs, dogs, and chickens before us, will one day be gone.

Did I say "silent"?

We are raucous. Jay, Penny, Tina and Naomi (Jay's girls), Bernie (Penny's mother), Joy, Victor, and Alyctra (now almost five), an architect, an author and his wife (a schoolteacher), their three sons, and myself. And two dogs. No one says a serious word. We are all comedians. Even the dogs are irreverent.

The "silence" is only a brief gasp before "grace" is once again omitted. But grace is implicit in this gathering, the sumptuous feast: turkey, dressing, mashed potatoes, garnets in orange cups (our author informs us that yams are grown only in Africa; what passes for yams here are usually garnets), rolls, assorted salads, cranberry sauce, gravy, Tina's British Trifle, pumpkin pie, cheesecake, and pecan fudge pie. We attack the feast in muffled exaltation.

When the food is largely demolished and we are up to the gills, we'd all like to find a quiet place to nap, animals that we are. Victor does it on the couch. It's hard for us on upright chairs.

By now I think Penny would like us to wash the dishes and leave quietly, but she is too polite. Only her whisper-of-mauve eyelids give her away. She still smiles and offers more food—like my Japanese mother would do.

At this time the author says, "Whoa-whoa-whoa. There's still business to attend to. There's still Bruce's homework."

"Homework on a holiday?" someone asks.

The schoolteacher says, "Well, Bruce (the youngest son—ten or eleven, I think) has to interview an older person for an oral report for his English class." You guessed it. Jay is the subject.

Jay turns alive. "Who, me?" He waves an open hand. "Not me. I've got no stories to tell. No, not me. You need someone..." He looks at me but doesn't say "older." His eyes almost cross from the restraint.

I suppose they're looking for walking-ten-miles-to-school-in-sleet-and-snow stories; catching-tadpoles-in-the-old-creek stories, water witching, trail blazing, before-the-wars (Grenada, Panama, Falklands, Vietnam, Korea, World War II) stories of prespace, pre-Nintendo days. (What do you do on cold winter nights? Snuff out the candles and bundle up, of course.)

Our personal Japanese American history reaches back only a generation before us. Our parents were immigrants from Japan, entering the United States as laborers. Some hopped the Mexican border illegally. Most settled in the West Coast states. Jay's folks went further east, winding their way through various occupations, including some nefarious business, before settling on a farm in Colorado. His father died there, leaving a widow with eight children. Jay is the youngest.

The widow moved her family to Los Angeles. Some of the children were already old enough to work; she herself shelled walnuts at home for twenty-five cents a bag and did not buy a new pair of shoes for thirteen years. Then, when the war with Japan happened, all Japanese and Japanese Americans on the West Coast were incarcerated for four years in camps located in the most desolate areas of the United States. And after the war, after the release from camp, the widow returned to Los Angeles with Jay, now almost a grown man. And there was his stint in the US Army before he met and married my sister.

Surely, some of that passes through Jay's mind, but maybe it's too complicated for a kid's school project. Our stories are locked in social and economic history. Maybe too painful. He insists: "I've got no stories to tell."

Joy and I have spent a lot of Christmases with Jay and have heard many of his stories. That's how I came to know some of this. Joy says quietly, "You have stories, Uncle Jay."

"No stories."

Joy and I speak together, "Tell the apple story!"

"Apple story?" Jay draws a blank. "What apple story?"

"The Christmas apple story," we say.

"I don't know no apple story." His eyes go off to search the past. He says hopefully, "I know an orange story."

How many fruit stories are there anyway? I'm reluctant to give up the apple story. It's so fragrant and juicy. But Joy says, "Okay, the orange story then." She's more flexible than I. Almost everyone is.

"Well, you know," Jay begins, "this is during the Depression. Know what a depression is, Bruce? It's no hole in the ground or dimple in your cheek. Depression's when people can't find jobs and there's no money around."

Bernie nods. I know she knows. Oh, yes.

Jay continues, "We're talking *no* money. And we're living in Colorado—our family—and, you know, not many orange groves in Colorado. It's Christmas, and we are poor. Real poor. But so is everyone else. I'm about, oh, four years old. My dad brings home a crate of oranges, a real treat. Not many orange trees in Colorado, did I mention? This is the first Christmas present I remember. A big navel orange. The bugger was this big." His strong hands circle the memory of his Christmas orange. He puts it to his nose and inhales mightily.

"They were big in those days," the architect agrees. "Whatever happened to those monster oranges?" I didn't think he was old enough to remember the giant navels.

Jay continues, "Each orange is wrapped in paper—sort of like tissue paper only stronger, slicker. Crackly. With a purple logo. Well, each of us gets an orange, and we sit around a long table. Like this one. All eight of us, yeah, eight kids from four on up to the teens sitting there with an orange in front." Jay sits like an emperor.

Family rituals are born this way. In a large, poor family, most presents are food items, and each gets the same gift, as nearly equal in size as possible. From old to young, the same, at the same time and at the table where everyone can see. There is no question of anyone not getting or getting smaller, fewer, or better. Then all eat at the same time. No one is encouraged to hold off for an hour or a day, later to wield power or arouse envy. Of course, even with these safeguards, there are tricks, trades, and sometimes even acts of generosity.

"First, you unwrap your orange," Jay says. He shows us how it's done, setting the wrapper on the table and smoothing it with the palms of his hands and laying the orange carefully on top. "Then you peel it."

He digs his thumb into the orange. "In those days, navel oranges had thick pulpy skins," he says.

There is no wrapper, no orange, no mother looking benignly on. Yet it's all there. I see the rind squirting oil and staining Jay's fingers. I smell it. I feel the mother's smile.

Jay looks to his siblings to see if he's doing it right. "You can't get too far ahead, or you'll finish too soon," he says. "Some of my sisters can peel it so it opens up like a lotus with the orange sitting in the middle like a jewel." He wipes his hands on his pants. "Now you take the peel, one piece at a time, and eat the white pulp."

Bruce barely reacts, but it doesn't get past Jay.

"Sure, it's not what you call tasty, but that's the beauty of it. That's what makes the orange so sweet. The reward. You scrape the peel with your lower teeth," he shows the mandible, "till you're right against the bitter rind."

The architect works his lower jaw. Was he also poor once? Maybe he just likes orange peels.

"Then you set the rind aside. Now you separate the sections. Each section is like a . . . a lover." Jay glances at the author, whose brows jerk stiffly.

"The flesh glistens and quivers with sweet juice. The membrane is a tissue. You peel it off and eat it along with the little strings that hang around." He pulls off the delicate strings with his pinkie lifted.

"And now, the orange. One by one. Not too fast. Can't get ahead of the game, you know." He looks furtively to his left and then to his right. "But in the end," he puts the sections in his mouth in rapid succession, "you can't help yourself, and you're the first to finish after all. But," he holds up a hand, "if you're a cute kid like me, one of your sisters will give you an extra piece or two."

Everyone laughs. "What happened to the rest of the oranges?" someone asks.

"Huh?"

"The extra oranges in the crate. What happened to them?"

"Beats me," Jay says. "My dad probably gave them away. He was like that. Always giving things away. Big shot."

The story is over. The author and the schoolteacher sit back and smile. The author asks his son to read what he's written. Bruce demurs. The schoolteacher thinks Bruce should hold an orange when he gives his report. "You don't have to peel it, honey," she says.

Bruce looks anxious. He shifts his feet. "It's only a school report," he says. He's a modest kid, and he doesn't want to stand out above the crowd. We can see his brain ticking. Maybe it's not such a good story. An orange for Christmas? Who'd believe it? They'd laugh at him. Take an orange to school and do all that stuff with the hands and the sniffing and all that? No way. Maybe the bell will ring before his turn comes around. Oh, God, he'd like to forget the whole thing. Maybe there'll be another fire.

The apple story is almost the same as the orange one. There is the smelling and the eating, but there is also the decision of when to eat it: while the apple is cracking fresh and exploding with juice? Eat it now, and there'll be no present on Christmas day. Wait till Christmas, and the apple is past its prime—dry and mealy. Will this be a group decision? Will Jay sneak off and eat his apple early and do the begging thing on Christmas?

The fruit is interchangeable. The story is appreciated only in retrospect. In remembrance. Maybe when Bruce has children of his own, he will pass it on. Well, maybe not. Can you hear them: "What? Not that old orange story again." They'd laugh at him.

Besides, how will he re-create the socioeconomic experience of the Japanese immigrants? Jay is probably Bruce's first contact with us. And he will have stories of his own: his author father and his teacher mother, who was always telling him how to do things better, and his brothers smirking in the back.

The story is rather grim and sad anyway. It speaks of adversity, of people building a network of support within walls: the family, the immigrant community. "Give the remaining oranges to the neighbor's kids." Still, it glows with warmth and courage and the innocence of another period.

But times change. Throw out the things that are no longer useful. So what if you never recapture the exact color of the sunset you remember. There will be other sunsets. Don't hang on to things. Forget the simple pleasures, the mother's eyes. Memory plays tricks. An era passes and never returns.

McNisei

Our tribe is fast disappearing, the Nisei, the first generation of American-born Japanese. They called us the "quiet Americans," the "model minority." Silence is being unseen, invisible—not to invite anger or envy. "The nail that sticks out gets hammered" is a saying more familiar to us than, say, "The squeaking wheel gets the oil."

Now, we Nisei are in our seventies and eighties. We did well after the camps. Most of us with Depression era experience set out immediately making up for lost time. We went to school, learned a trade, and salted away or invested our wages so we should not have to be poor and powerless again.

Well, it wasn't exactly like that with me. My typing and office skills were poor to middling, and I spent a lot of productive years in factories on my feet. My big ambition was to get a job that required a lot of sitting. I didn't stash away a mattress full of money, but thanks to lucky timing, social security, and some clever budgeting, I got by. So I cannot be included in the "most" that lined comfortable nests for later.

But that's all right because now, in our retirement, we have no need to be so competitive among ourselves: to get better grades than thee; to work at that upscale job, drive the flashy car, have more money, to be more "white" than thee. Without our jobs (sure, we still have our prestige cars; that car thing is hard to shake), but in our sweatpants and walking shoes, we are all one of a bunch—all Nisei.

At last, we are comfortable with that. Our cultural foods are widely accepted, and our language is seeping into everyday English: sushi, sukiyaki, tempura, panko, Honda, Toyota, Mitsubishi, karioki, harry-cary, and like that. The last two are American pronunciations. It's not important that you know the literal translations. We know. If it matters to you: *karaoke* means empty orchestra, that is, without a vocalist; and *hara-kiri* is a respected form of suicide: a knife to the belly.

Now we seek one another's company and enjoy the Japanese American language, the puns and jokes that, when translated, make no sense. We let the clichés roll. We like clichés; they make us feel closer to white America (nearer, my God, to Thee).

We older ones trade tough-time stories. We have chewed the hard heel of an old loaf of bread and have grown to like it. Those of us over seventy-five remember the taste of bread mold. We have worn hand-me-downs; we know the feel of cardboard in our shoes and the fullness of rice sloshed down with tea. We call it *chazuke,* our soul food, our heritage, along with the better-known sashimi and the *ondo* (street dancing) and a "can-do" attitude. *Gambare* is our call to arms.

Gardena is fifteen miles southwest of downtown Los Angeles. Before the war it was an enclave of Japanese farmers; after the war, many Nisei returned to Gardena, maybe to be with one another again. We Nisei retirees have a few assembly points here. Those I know of are Bob's Okazuya, the Marukai food court, Rainbow Donuts, the McDonald's on Redondo Beach and Normandie, another on Artesia and Normandie, and one on Crenshaw and Redondo as well. This last one isn't so prime: too many students from El Camino College sitting around nursing coffees, buried in books, or ragging each other.

Our group congregates each weekday morning on Redondo Beach and Normandie. Diehards come on weekends, too. At our particular location, there are factions: Those from Hawai'i gather against a low partition on the east side of the restaurant on a long bench and small tables; they face the morning sun. The fishermen congregate in two booths on the west wall, the golfers occupy another booth on the same wall, and we take the middle bench against another low partition with tables that accommodate, say, ten or twelve. Our group is the largest and has members with the most varied interests.

Many of our men (and some women) are technologists with plenty of computer smarts—expert downloaders and stuff. Almost all are gourmets (actually eaters with knowledge of eateries along the California coast). Many are *karaoke* singers or aficionados. We also have a couple of tennis players. We have a lot of gamblers. Every group has gamblers—not hard core. We are casino people, mostly slot players and a few tough crap shooters and big-time blackjackers.

Golfers sometimes join us. The fishermen hardly ever do, but they are friendly and often pass homemade goodies (tofu pie, brownies) to us. We do the same.

"You take food to McDonald's?" you might ask. It was a tradition established years before I joined the group: If you won at the casino, you brought donuts for everyone, yes, to McDonald's. If you lost (everyone knew where you'd been), you crawled in (figuratively) with your hands cupped outward. If you took a trip, say, to Alaska and caught a salmon, you smoked it and brought a portion to McDonald's.

At first, I wasn't comfortable with taking food to a restaurant, but the counter people did not seem to mind, and often the extras were passed on to them. At Christmas we always took up a collection for them.

Ours is a warm family-type group. We tease one another, make jokes (the older we get, the raunchier and more graphic, you know what I mean?) But most Nisei don't care for notoriety. I don't know how to tell this story without implicating some very recognizable names, but I feel these are the last chapters of our Nisei book, and someone should tell the stories before they are lost. Along with the vapor of our breath. But, what the heck; in a few years no one will remember us or care.

George and his wife are well known in these parts; he was an elected school board member some years back. He and Iku are educators and belong to a lot of social and political organizations. They are founders of a well-known Japanese American group. I'd heard the organization was working on a book on the resettlement (after-camp) years, and I wanted to write for it. I found that George and Iku lived on my block, and, not without strategy, I attended a meeting at their house, made new friends, and the society accepted my story and my membership. Though I can't say the rest is history, it was certainly the beginning of a fine friendship.

George is retired; Iku still works. She is too young for retirement, and, though God knows they are both busy with meetings and activities,

George, since his retirement, had been walking a mile or two around the neighborhood every morning. He invited me to join him.

George and I fell into the middle group at McDonald's on Normandie and Redondo. In our walks, we had slipped into the habit of stopping for coffee breaks, here, there, and finally at McDonald's. McDonald's offered a twenty-seven-cent coffee to seniors, multiple refills, and air conditioning. And free refreshments—a win-win deal.

After a week or so, a McNisei (George coined the name) recognized George and invited us to join them. They welcomed us like they'd been waiting for us the whole eight or ten years of congregating. George, with his academic and political background, tells a lot of hilarious stories of his experiences. And there are other talkers, teasers, insulters, and just plain listeners. It's great fun. A jolt of caffeine and a couple of laughs are not a bad way to start the day.

Because George and I came in together, some of the regulars thought we were married. Only George is married, I explained, and not to me. I am obviously older than George, and if you talk to him long enough, you'd know he's a devoted husband. I'm divorced. And if you talked to me long enough, you'd probably surmise why. But that's beside the point.

Not many divorced women of my age come to our McDonald's. Not many women, period. Well, some widows, a couple of us divorcees, just a few wives but they are not regular McNisei. I am one of the women who come regularly because I don't do aerobics, crafts, line dancing, card games, or have other distracting activities (one widow is a member of an exercise group, a card club, and four singles clubs. I'll talk about her later). I am the only true dud there.

One morning, by coincidence, a lot of women showed up, and I said, "Look, we're in the majority today."

Hide was just walking in. "Good!" she said. "Let's vote on something."

Hide is Tak's wife. Tak is one of the old-timers, probably the first McNisei. George calls him the chairman of the board. Tak uses his tongue like a whip. You don't really belong until you've been insulted by him. He sits in his special chair and doles out caustic comments to whomever is in shooting range. "You made this at home, eh?" he might ask, biting into a cookie. "Well, you should have left it there." Or, "If you don't want the truth, you gonna get it anyway."

Hide tells me he used to embarrass her with his straight talk, but, after a while, she decided, heck, *she* didn't bring him up, that was his mother's job. And it's too late now anyway.

When Tak is absent, a strange phenomenon occurs: whoever takes his seat changes in a heartbeat: a sly smile slips over his face, and the biting words flow out. Even George, normally quite congenial, clapped his hand over his mouth one day and said, "What am I saying? I'm not like this!" and quickly moved to another seat. Pastor Paul doesn't actually have to sit in the chair; one near enough will do. Maybe he's more susceptible because he's purer than the average guy. I've noticed the pastor's usually kind manner develops an edge, in fun, of course, but I know that wicked smile.

The pastor likes to fish and often wears a jacket with many pleated pockets, a floppy hat or a snow cap, or even shorts, depending on the weather. He looks like the rest of us. People don't immediately remember that he is a genuine Lutheran pastor. Those that enjoy cussing or taking the Lord's name in vain continue to do so, and Interneters pass around sheets of downloaded off-color jokes right in front of him. When I look to see his reaction, he nods as though to say, "Good stuff for Sunday's sermon." Actually, I don't really know; I've never been to his church. And Pastor Paul doesn't recruit at McDonald's.

Tak's father, an immigrant from Japan, started his life here as a coal miner and bachelor in Idaho. Then he married the cousin of a fellow miner. He worked on the railroad in Utah, then moved to Southern California, where he joined a tuna boat in San Pedro. For whatever reason, he then moved to a farm in Costa Mesa, then farmed again in Hawthorne.

Tak got his wanderlust and self-confidence from his father. He is unafraid of change. Tak has variously (not chronologically) worked at dental labs, been a landlord several times, opened a laundromat, invested in a Chinese restaurant, sold insurance, and, I suppose, had a couple of other jobs.

Hide and Tak have been married close to fifty years. After camp Hide relocated to Cleveland, hoping to support herself while attending college, but the stress wore her out. Since work came first, she let the college go. She married Tak, and, after four children, she went to work as a medical transcriber. That takes smarts. She listened to the dictaphone and typed out medical reports. It wasn't easy with doctors with foreign or regional accents drawling their words over those hard-to-spell diseases and pharmaceutical terms. And she had to be accurate.

Hide quit that job and later helped Tak with his insurance work. The paperwork. The tedious stuff. Through the years her health faltered, but she maintained her grace and sense of humor. I love that.

Example: One morning Charlie, who usually gets in late, sat at a separate table and seemed to be waiting for something. He often buys pancakes, eggs, and a muffin, and carefully cuts everything, including the muffin, into bite-sized pieces, methodically following a mental grid. After this ritual, he eats, one small square at a time. By this time the food is cold, but each little piece waits in line for its turn at the eating machine. They tell me Charlie was an engineer before retirement.

This morning Charlie sat at another table and just waited. Tak reminded him that there are no waiters at McDonald's. "You have to get in line to order," he said.

Charlie shot him a "puh-leeze" look. Then he said, "I know that. I'm waiting for a friend. We're going out for breakfast." That's what we McNisei did—waited for friends at McDonald's and ate elsewhere.

Tak offered, "At the Normandie Club, you can get a nice piece of ham, two eggs, potatoes, and toast for $2.29. And the coffee is free."

"Is that right?" Charlie asked and studied the Normandie menu in his head. Charlie is a visual man. His eyes rolled up. "Let's see," he said, "ham...two eggs...potatoes comma...."

Hide and I fell out laughing. No one understood what was so funny, not even Charlie.

Later, when I told this to my friend (the writer), she didn't laugh either. "Would you have put a semicolon there?" I asked. "A dash, perhaps?"

"No," she said, "a comma is fine, providing it isn't the end of a sentence."

"Well," I said, "Hide and I had a good laugh over it. I guess you had to be there." "That might help," my friend said.

The seat across from Tak is Fred's. He's our oldest, and he has taken over as our Lothario. He likes to lean over women and whisper sweet dirties to them. His wife, when she comes, enjoys his merriment. Missy is very polite and laughs at anything even remotely funny.

Fred is also Tak's foil, like Abbot's Costello, if you remember them. Fred usually sits across from Tak, and he gets it full force and accepts it without rancor. "Heh-heh, that right? Well, have you heard this one then?" And he goes on to tell another joke. Tak might say, "Yeah, yesterday. And the week before, too."

It's true. All the stories we tell have long lives. But I've seen Tak patiently listen to some that I myself have heard three or four times. And I'm a relative newcomer, too.

One morning Lila came in without her boyfriend. Lila's the widow with memberships in four singles clubs. Tak's comment about that: "Four clubs and you could only snare one man? Not a good average." Lila wears T-shirts with huge silkscreened lilacs sprinkled with sequins or beads. Her clothes always scream out, "Hey! It's me!"

Lila, like me, is on the far side of seventy. You can see that she was once a stunner, and you know the same pretty face has been looking back at her from her mirror day after day, year after year, never changing, feeding back an implanted image. That happened to me, too. Not that I was such a beauty, but I got in the habit of seeing the same face in the mirror and somehow missed the subtle changes that were happening—wrinkles that had sneaked in, hair that had turned gray and was thinning. Then one day I saw myself reflected on a shop window and I gasped, "Who are you, old lady?" That was my reality check.

Lila wears three sparkling earrings on each ear and as many rings on her ravaged fingers (rheumatoid arthritis). In summer she might wear a crocheted midriff blouse without a bra (too hot, she says), or a chiffon mid-ankle dress and usually a lacy little wrap draped over her spotted arms. This is at McDonald's in mid-morning.

And Lila is serenely confident that the world revolves around her. She let us know this when her worst complaint about the camp experience was that the guys were going out on work leave or volunteering for the army, and chances for dates were pretty thin. She accepts that all eyes automatically turn to her when she enters McDonald's (and they do) and that the only thing that interests any one of us is the state of Lila.

One morning she plopped onto the empty chair next to Tak and sighed, "It's such a chore to come here every morning."

This was an easy one for Tak. "Don't come then," he said.

"Well," she said, "I don't like to drink my coffee alone." That explained everything, of course. Then she laughed and proceeded to tell three stories, one right after the other: the hat-check girl, the little-hole-big-hole, and the Las Vegas rubber stories. I won't explain any of them except to say she was the star in each, and the stories were racy and absolutely word for word just as I heard them the first, second, and third times. In the same breathless voice. Nothing, no detail omitted.

While these tales were being spun out, I watched Tak's face. He smiled stiffly, waited for the punch line, and laughed politely. Only one twitching eyelid revealed his unwilling participation in this playlet.

This was a new side of Tak. I could learn a little kindness and patience from him, I thought. But he got even with her later. Lila has a habit of brushing against guys when she gets up. This time she touched Tak's arm with her fingers. He said, "Your hands are cold. Are you still alive?"

But Lila would not take offense. I think that's part of being loved from early on. She's confident she is adored by all.

I wouldn't call Paul (not the pastor) a tough customer. He is a Kenny Rogers type but younger and better looking, married, but he comes alone most of the time. Once, way back before my time, Lila offended Paul, and he has not forgiven her. He shows her by throwing hard looks or sighing with exasperation when she falls against him. I think Lila considers him a challenge; she smiles almost triumphantly at these times. We watch the maneuvers with rapt attention. What else to do?

Shoji sat next to Tak until early spring. Shoji is a former martial arts instructor and a *kiatsu* (acupressure) expert. He worked first as an army recruiter in Hawai'i and later as a postal worker and a night manager at McDonald's. Ours. He teaches crafts at the senior center. He also sings, plays the ukulele, and can be contacted for parties, weddings, installations, any festivity. He is always ready to buy coffee or anything else you might want: Waffles? An Egg McMuffin? Hash browns? Anything. And regardless of who brings what, he always orders a biscuit for himself, as though that might make up for all the food we don't order at McDonald's.

Shoji is from Hawai'i, but he sits with us and only visits with the Hawai'i people. Among us, he is the one most likely to enter sainthood; he never speaks ill of anyone except to tease. When he hears negative stuff, he smiles as if his hearing aid isn't working. You know that look. When my daughter sees it on me, she asks, "You didn't hear me, did you?"

Shoji is the kind of guy that will give you acupressure wherever you hurt; yes, right there at McDonald's. He fixed the pain in my heel before I got to the podiatrist, so I was able to cancel my appointment and save myself a lot of time and money. And he gave me two beautiful leis that he had designed and made. I gave him only my obsequious thanks.

Then one day Shoji got seriously ill, and, after a critical operation, he was out for over half a year. For most of us this is a scary thing. These are crucial years. Who will be next?

There were others who came and left before George and I joined. One was a wonderful woman who organized hospital visits and took up collections for flowers and cards for sick people. When she herself fell ill, she wouldn't allow flowers or visits, and she quietly died alone at the hospital. Hide took up the floral collection for Shoji's convalescence.

This year, sometime in late spring, McDonald's suddenly announced that the senior coffee price was to be discontinued. Coffee jumped from twenty-seven cents to a dollar and seven cents. We were shocked. Some checked the other McDonald's owned by the same man (he has four franchises) and reported that ours was the only one whose senior price was terminated. On the counter was a large sign: "SENIOR COFFEE DISCONTINUED." And by the coffee dispenser: "REFILLS FOR DINERS ONLY." Obviously the boss wanted us out. Why? We didn't take up that much space. There were always plenty of tables for "real" customers.

Most of us agreed that McDonald's had been patient with us: ten years of cheap coffee, a meeting place, and carrying in our own refreshments. Maybe we should have been more considerate. Paid rent or something. Still we were singled out, and that hurt.

Pastor Paul offered the kitchen at his church. He said, "We have tables, chairs, a big coffee pot and everything. You can make your own coffee." Yeah, and wash out the pot and cups, and sweep up the crumbs, and take home the dish towels to wash. I could see us women again scurrying about in a kitchen. No, that wouldn't do.

Then we considered picketing. "Unfair to seniors!"; "Senior discount revoked!"; or, my favorite: "Hell no, we won't go!" We'd be hanging in there as coffee prices jumped to five dollars a cup. Or "Racist!" That one didn't wash.

But picketing didn't get past the talking stage. I guess it was the summer heat and the street traffic. The monoxide level on a weekday—hey, that's hazardous to our health. We might as well all start smoking again.

The Hawai'i group on the east wall moved to the McDonald's on Artesia and Normandie. Their senior coffee is thirty-nine cents. The fishermen on the west wall grumbled but weren't inclined to action; the golfers disappeared. But we in the middle stood our ground and tried to meet with the owner: He wouldn't meet. We then decided that George, since he is the most distinguished of us, would write a letter to the *Gardena Valley News*. It was a reasonable letter asking why we were singled out to be denied the senior price. George hand-delivered it to the editor. The paper didn't print it. George sent the same letter to the owner. He didn't respond.

Then, right in the middle of summer, George was called back to work, and none of the rest of us had the pluck or polish to pursue it further.

It's winter now. We've adjusted to the coffee price. We hardly feel the pain any more. Well, there are some who still go to the counter and ask for senior coffee and are met with "That'll be a dollar seven, please."

For a while some of the Hawai'i group dropped by on their way to the post office, which is on the same block. They missed "home," they said. Robert and Ray from that group, joined us permanently. At first they sat quietly on the far side. Now they are integrated. Not entirely true. Ray hardly comes anymore. Tak says his wife won't let him drive.

"Ray's losing it," Tak says. I couldn't tell. Once when someone mentioned Alzheimer's, Ray had said, "We all have Alzheimer's." I thought that was quite observant—and undeniable.

Shoji has returned to us. He has lost weight. He is subdued. But he smiles. And he still gets to his feet to buy coffee for others. Not quick enough any more. He's still healing. He used to tell stories of picking *oogoo* (seaweed) off the rocks in Hawai'i, but he's not fast enough to finish three sentences before being interrupted. We have become impatient. Too many stories to tell yet, and too little time. But we are all happy to see him, including the counter people. I think Shoji's happy, too.

One morning a few of us decided to have breakfast at nearby Carrow's. There were Hide and Tak, Fred and Missy, and me. I was the last of our group to leave McDonald's when Lila teetered by without her boyfriend.

"Where're you going?" she asked.

I told her we were going to Carrow's for breakfast and asked if she cared to join us. It must have been a lonely day for her; she was quick. By the time I got to Carrow's parking lot, she was already out of her car.

Lila sat in the middle of the curved booth and appointed herself in charge. She talked without pause. And Missy was goading her on. Missy isn't a frequent McNisei, so she hadn't heard these stories before. "How can she remember all this?" she asked with great admiration. "By repetition!" I wanted to scream.

Then Lila's talk took a serious turn. You know how it is when you're on a roll. You go on and on and suddenly find yourself in deep water. Then it's too late to stop or retract.

Lila told us that her father left the family when she was eleven and never returned. Her mother was an enterprising young woman, and, with two kids to support, she started a business in Little Tokyo. Lila called it something in Japanese; I'm not familiar with the term.

Lila continued, "Oh, my mother used to play the *shamisen* and sing. She dressed up, you know. She wore Japanese kimonos. All dressed up. And in those days they used to give her gold coins."

"Who gave her gold coins?" I asked.

"The customers. The men gave her gold coins," Lila said impatiently. "I had a bunch of them made into a bracelet. She made good money. She served food, too."

By that time I got an inkling of the nature of her mother's business. I told myself not to jump to conclusions, but the atmosphere of men, smoke-filled rooms, drinking, entertainment, laughter, good times, and gold coins prevailed. It sort of drowned out Lila's sense of loss for a runaway father.

Now it becomes clearer why Lila pokes three sparkling earrings in each ear every morning and meticulously selects her wardrobe to make her entrance at McDonald's. Her hair is always scrupulously auburn, cut in carefree unisex, never showing gray roots. Maybe it is a chore to attend to it all.

But this is Lila's commitment: to attract, to entertain, to be resourceful and ever cheerful. It's a family tradition. (Does the apple always have to fall so close to the tree? Well, the thistle rides the wind and aspires to other climes.)

Lila was just over twenty when she married. Her two children are now grown, doing well, and have kids of their own. Her husband had the temerity to die while she was in the hospital getting knee replacements for those legs that had been voted (she told us twice) the most beautiful in Poston, a camp with ten thousand inmates.

"I was in the hospital, for God's sake, couldn't move, couldn't do anything, and he died on me!" she said. Sort of like her father, who had abandoned her when she needed him most. At least her husband had the decency to depart after the children were grown.

But it's okay. Everything worked out fine. Unlike her father, Lila's husband left her with plenty of money. No need for gold coins here.

That was a few years back. Her knees have long since healed, her finances are in good order, and her boyfriend is nine years younger. Together they have traveled the world over: Paris, Tokyo, Moscow, wherever. Having fun is no easy job, don't you know? Boy, the lies we live to keep the true lies buried. But I would say she has retained her optimism, and that's plenty to admire.

Family Gifting

They say family stories are like Christmas newsletters. Boring. But I want to get this one down because, way later, my grandkids might want to read something like this and try to connect with it. I see them today: they have all they could want to eat and most of what they think they need to be happy. Maybe they would want to know how all the abundance evolved from stark lives only two generations back.

This thought came to me last year, just a week before Christmas, when Alyctra and Lucas still hadn't decided what they wanted from Grammy. That's what my grandkids call me. Early on, I asked not to be called "Granny." It conjures up a toothless old hag hobbling about on a cane, and, while it's true that I'm old, I don't use a cane (yet) and I do have all my teeth. Well, 90 percent.

Alyctra and Lucas call their dad's mother "Ba-chan," which is an affectionate Japanese term for grandma. Once Lucas called me "Ba-chan," and, when I reminded him I was "Grammy," he immediately apologized. "Oh, I love you both so much, I get you mixed up," he said.

That was a few years ago. I thought it was quick thinking for a kid in preschool; I mean, he could have said, "Sometimes I get you mixed up because you're both so old and forgetful." Yes, that was in his vocabulary. Or cranky.

But Ba-chan isn't cranky. She was raised in Japan and is sweet and patient, as most Japanese women of that era are. She was born in Los Angeles, but when she turned four, the family moved back to Japan. Later they were among those who colonized Manchuria.

Ba-chan speaks only Japanese. And she doesn't do a whole lot of talking like I do. Often she appears to acquiesce, but in truth, she is strong and stoic. Once she told me of hiding in the attic when the Russians invaded Manchuria. It was toward the end of World War II, in August of 1945, when Japan had already surrendered to America, but the Russians continued to march into Manchuria, looting and marauding. And, of course, raping. But Ba-chan didn't say that in so many words.

She was probably in her late teens then and very pretty, with curly black hair. She and her family had hidden in the attic, barely breathing, not daring to stretch a cramped knee until they were sure the soldiers had moved on, taking with them all they could carry, including the pot of cold rice. She told me this when we were in my kitchen scraping off the dinner plates. We had just finished dinner. "What a waste," she said as I started the garbage disposal. The ghost of that pot of cold rice still lived.

A sense of Ba-chan's past comes out like that, bit by bit, often when we are busy setting up the table or chopping vegetables for a family dinner. Ba-chan follows me around helping with whatever I'm doing. We're contemporaries. Other family members are younger, and some are Americans of different ethnicity.

I was born and raised in America, too, but I speak a little Japanese, and that and our age connects Ba-chan to me. I try to piece her stories together as I rush around, but I'm not familiar with her Kagoshima dialect, and also she speaks so softly I don't quite catch all the details. In these flashes of her life, she seems to be asking, "Tell me what was it all for?" I told Ba-chan she should write these stories down, after all they are the grandkids' history, but she said, "Oh, I can't write."

Ba-chan is comfortable in America now and though Ji-chan (Grandpa) died and these past few years have been lonely ones for her, today, I don't think there is a thing or a condition that she fears. Not poverty or age. . Perhaps not even death. Only the question remains: "What was it all for?" Maybe Alyctra and Lucas can answer that for her one day, but later. Later.

Now about Ji-chan: He was born in Japan and had immigrated to America before World War II. He, like the rest of us Japanese and Japanese Americans living on the West Coast, spent the war in a concentration camp; I suppose he lived in the bachelors' quarters with other single men from Japan. After we were released from camp, he was determined not to be a workaday gardener anymore; he decided to take up landscaping. He learned to speak English grammatically; he threw out the Japanese accent. He learned the Latin words for all the flora, and he studied books on designing and plumbing and all that goes with getting a landscaper's license. He took the examination seven times before he finally passed. He was proud of that.

He himself didn't tell me when or how he met and married Ba-chan. My daughter Joy said it was after Ba-chan's family left Manchuria and returned to Japan. The marriage was arranged by relatives or friends, and Ba-chan met Ji-chan through an exchange of pictures. These two strong-willed people decided to accept one another and were married in Japan by proxy. Ba-chan then came to America to be with her husband.

I don't think it was easy, but over the years they learned to trust and rely on one another. They had two boys.

Joy married Victor, the eldest son. They met while they were both working at the catering business that belonged to my late ex-husband, Joy's father. Joy also taught elementary classes in cultural diversity (until Governor Reagan cut the state budget for it). Victor became a dentist, and Joy was promoted to stay at home with Alyctra and Lucas.

Alyctra is familiar with the history of the Japanese internment in America. She loves to read, and Joy often steers the direction so Alyctra has a fair knowledge of it. Yes, the incarceration was a huge shock to the Japanese Americans even though we thought we knew the big and small of racism. Our share of "liberty and justice for all" had its limits, but we were politically naive and believed in America's promise.

I have sometimes relived those camp years in my dreams, often crossing vast deserts and seas of wind-swept sage, and, upon arriving at the familiar complex of tar-paper barracks, I have found only ghostly forms walking the dusty streets. Maybe one of them is me. The dreams are haunting and lonely, but they are not like the nightmares Ba-chan has endured. I don't know the trauma of invasion, of life hanging on the stillness of a shallow breath.

In my "after camp," I met a young man whose family lived in the city before and after camp. He was a gregarious guy. In that respect (and a few others), we were total opposites, which wasn't a good sign, but in our headstrong youth we thought we could overcome all problems.

My husband was still in school; I worked in various factories to pay the bills. The living was not easy. After graduation, my husband found a job in a Japanese employment agency. This seemed suited to his nature, and he was happy with talking and helping people into jobs. We started a family with our Joy.

There were many Nisei just out of camp looking for work then. People shared rooms in hostels with communal kitchens or lived with other families in crowded rentals; some slept in garages or lean-tos and used a family's bathroom. Like the immigrant Latinos do now. I never once heard anyone complain or say he or she wanted to go back to camp. But in the National Archives there is a picture of an old man hanging from a ceiling beam on the last day of camp. Maybe he couldn't take the defeat of his beloved Japan. Maybe outside life was too frightening.

Jobs were discriminatory. The agency mostly got requests for domestic help: live-in maids, chauffeurs, butlers, cooks, servers, low-level assembly work. My husband was on commission, but before long taking money from talented, alert Nisei for placing them in such menial, humbling jobs began to gnaw on him. To assuage his guilt, he took guys to lunch or brought them home, sometimes inviting them (one at a time, of course) to stay for days. Weeks. And one even months. That's the kind of man he was.

With housekeeping, washing diapers, sterilizing, cooking, nursing a colicky baby, attending to guests, and suffering from postpartum blues, I looked forward to rest in a nice, quiet asylum. But I just couldn't break down. Once, at one of many informal gatherings at our house, a friend remarked that my husband was one of the kindest and most generous men he'd ever known.

"Yes," I agreed, "it's true; he is kind and generous. He'd give you the shirt off my back." No one laughed.

No matter how we strained the budget, my husband always made sure that Joy got what she wanted. One Christmas she fell in love with a doll she saw on television. Betsy Wetsy could drink from a bottle and wet her diapers.

At the store, I found a doll twice the size of Betsy for half the price, with rooted hair and eyelashes and movable eyes. She wore a dress and panties; no diapers for this baby. I thought my husband would be delighted with my find. He said, "That's not what Joy wants. Take it back and get a Betsy Wetsy."

After dolls came fishes and turtles, one hamster, cats and dogs. And there was a time of horses too. Joy kept a stable of plastic horses, families of them in plastic barns, fences, faux leather saddles, and things. Gifting was easy then.

In time, my husband quit the agency. He found himself a chef and started a catering business. Slowly the business grew. Joy grew. And one year she wanted a real horse. "Forget it," I said. "Put it out of your mind."

Joy said, "If it costs too much, I'll pay for part of it." That's the kind of kid she was. She was already working part-time for her father and getting minimum wage so she had money.

"Joy," I said, "that's just part of the problem. I'm thinking, renting a stable in the country, and you know Daddy works weekends so I'll be the one driving you out there every weekend. I'm thinking, sitting all day parked in a pasture waiting for you." I've always been afraid of horses.

"You could take a book," she said.

"Yeah," I said. "Hundreds of them. How long do you think an average horse lives?" Bet she never thought of that.

She smiled. "Ask Daddy," she said. I think she actually believed that he would bring her a horse that Christmas. But he didn't.

Joy is our only child, and she had it easy compared to kids in large families or even ones with as few as two. Take Victor and his brother. They were both born in December, a year and a few days apart and very close to Christmas, so friends and family who were inclined to give gifts found it hard to come up with two presents for each of them. Victor remembers best the year a relative gave them one tennis racquet and one ball for both of them. They took turns hitting the ball against the house. Thunka-thunka-thunka. Now that would drive me crazy.

Joy told me that story. Victor, like his father, doesn't talk much about personal stuff. My father was quiet, and my brother is too. My husband was different; he was a city boy and loved people, loved to laugh and give things. Me, I have always been into myself (from the get-go, my mother often said); I learned to enjoy my resourcefulness, to make do or do without. There's pleasure in that too.

In Joy's own household, she celebrates all holidays. Thanksgiving, Christmas, New Year's, birthdays, Valentine's, Saint Patrick's, Easter, Girls' Day, Boys' Day, Mother's and Father's Days—you get the picture. It's like an obsession. Once I asked her if I'd given her enough presents when she was a child. Well, I may have asked more than once because she said, "I wish you'd stop asking that."

Ba-chan gives the children money for most of these occasions, or she cooks a festive dish for them. Since Ji-chan passed away and she doesn't drive, this seems to work fine with her. But I'm not a great cook, and I've never gotten used to passing out money. I have a hard time with that. Oh, sure, Joy sometimes buys the presents and I write her a check later. Hey, it's not the same. It's more duplicitous.

I try not to do that too often, but as you may have guessed, shopping isn't my favorite thing. After my husband and I split, I've been alone on these exhilarating excursions, and I usually keep them short and dry.

Sometimes I ask the kids directly what they want, and sometimes I ask in questions loaded with clumsy deceitful turns, but they're on to me. They know I'm a bah-humbug person; they put up with my ruses or throw out detours of their own.

Maybe it was one of those times at the supermarket last year. The store was decorated for the holidays, and shelves were loaded with toys and candy. On a high ledge in the veggie department, there was a line-up of giant teddy bears wearing velvet Christmas bows. The shelf was not at eye-level, and it was in the grocer's section so neither Alyctra nor Lucas noticed the bears.

The kids followed Joy and me around as we pushed through the aisles thinking substance: meat, bread, potatoes. Every now and then Lucas would get excited and pick up a toy, and I'd ask, "Is that what you want for Christmas?" And he'd say, "Just looking, Grammy." Alyctra was disinterested; there is nothing in a supermarket she'd care to be seen wearing.

Moments later, Lucas had quietly wandered away from us. When we found him, he was hugging a giant plush bear that had taken a break from the shelf above the spinach and turnips and was sitting on a stack of canned sodas in reach of every able-bodied child. He had removed his red velvet tie. Lucas hollered, "Grammy! Grammy! This is what I want for Christmas!"

"No, you don't," Joy said very quickly.

"Yes, yes, this is what I want," he screamed. Eureka! I thought. Joy was embarrassed.

"I'll get it for him," I said.

"No, he doesn't want it. He'll forget about it tomorrow," Joy said.

"Please let me get it for him," I said. "I want to make at least one person happy this Christmas."

"He's too big for it."

"Obviously he still has a need for it," I said.

Joy turned to Lucas. "Lucas, for that kind of money, you can get a computer game. You know that'd be more fun."

"I don't *want* a computer game," he wailed. "I want this bear."

"Look at it," Joy said. "It's all soiled with crust from kids' noses, crumbs from their crackers, and saliva and stuff; you don't want it."

Lucas said, "Yes, this is the one I want. I want *this* one. Everybody's hugged this one. This is the one I want."

Wow. That's deep.

Joy turned to me, "Believe me, I know him; he'll forget all about it tomorrow."

"If I don't get it for him, he will never forget this Christmas." I was on a roll.

Joy said, "I'm telling you: he'll get over it. Look at me, I didn't get the pony I wanted, and I got over it."

"You *didn't* get over it," I said very slowly. She was quiet.

All the while we were arguing, Alyctra was looking from one to the other. Then she put her arm around me.

"Look," I said, "I'll call Lucas tomorrow, and, if he still wants the bear, I'll get it. Okay?" I turned to Alyctra and asked, "Is there anything special I can get you for Christmas?"

"I want a pony," she whispered.

Was she putting me on? Or was she saying there are dreams that no one can ever fulfill for you? Or did she already know that the past is set in stone?

Shigin

Maybe this story should be written in Japanese, but since I'm telling the story, I can use only the language I know. Still, I have difficulties with syntax and vocabulary and using a lot of clichés, but those are clues to my roots.

Also, I don't really know all the facts; I've only observed from the outside, so I shall be drawing my own conclusions—connecting the dots, so to speak. My friend, a writer, once told me that when one writes the first word on paper, the story becomes fiction. I shall take comfort in that.

My parents were immigrants from Japan and though they tried to keep their American-born children in touch with the old country culture, after we started American school, our teachers told us to speak only English at school and at home. Of course, that last order wasn't possible to carry out, but, as years passed and with our successive generations, memories of Japanese and Japanese ways faded, and we did eventually speak only English at home.

Some customs like the *obon odori* (street dancing) have continued through the years, and sushi, teriyaki, and tempura are accepted nationally, but that is largely because of their popularity with other Americans, too. Particularly after World War II and the American occupation of Japan put an end to the antimiscegenation laws.

Then intermarriages surged, and mixed-race children *(hapa)* changed the color of our tight-knit Japanese American communities. In my time interracial children were quite rare, but, within two generations, the color and physicality (height and shape) of our people changed radically.

In our time, there were so few mixed-race children we were experts at identifying our *hapa* peers. We also knew kids among us that were from Japan. We called them FOBs—Fresh Off the Boat—patronizing, yes, but later it became just a way of identification. Although few people today choose to travel by boat, we sometimes still use the phrase.

My grandkids don't seem to know the difference between races even though their grandmother from Japan took care of them until preschool. Even though they learned to speak her language. Lucas and Alyctra are now ten and sixteen respectively. Alyctra is in an advanced Japanese-language class in high school, and Lucas is taking a Japanese-language class on Saturdays. They wanted to do this.

Last week we two grandmothers were invited to attend Lucas' New Year's program. The year before, the children mostly sang and recited in Japanese, but with a new principal the program took on a classy look. The logic was that, with only fifty or so Saturdays in a year, it was too costly to take off study time for rehearsals, so help from classic dance classes and other sources filled the program and gave it a professional air. There were *taiko* (drum) dancers in spectacular costumes, dancing and beating their drums in perfect synchrony, *koto* (a kind of horizontal harp) players with original music, and teachers participating in fun games on stage.

Now, we're talking about a small Japanese American cultural center in a small town: a cluster of classroom buildings—no real auditorium. Down in the basement of one structure, there was a long hall with an attached kitchen and two restrooms. On this day, the stage was a group of tables put together with a large runner thrown over to hold it all together. There was also a movable set of stairs leading to the stage. The sound equipment was put on stage for technicians to hop up and make adjustments when needed. Homey. Intimate.

A potluck buffet was held in this basement hall. Lunch was served first; Japanese outdo themselves with potluck. The food was plentiful and delicious. Our family was among the early arrivals, so we sat at the table closest to the stage—we two grandmothers, Lucas (who was soon running about with his friends), and Joy and Victor, his mother and father. Alyctra, Lucas' sister, was attending a meeting. She would join us later.

I noticed a stunning young man in costume standing against the wall near our seats. He wore a *hakama*, a form of formal Japanese men's wear: a black kimono top with a crest on the back worn with white undergarments showing smartly at the neckline and under the loose kimono sleeves. The wide pleated brocade trousers just barely showed the white *tabi* (formal socks) and *geta* (wooden clogs with cleats). *Hapa,* I thought. It was automatic.

The program said he was Ban-sensei (teacher Ban), the host. Ban-sensei introduced the performers in flawless Japanese and then introduced them again in just as flawless English. Wow. I read the program. He was also to sing *shigin.*

Shigin, Ban-sensei explained, was a form of music set to poems and classical tales. Well, it's music, yes, but not the toe-tapping melodic stuff we're used to. *Shigin* is a classic art form that takes years of study to perfect. The vocal chords must be in total control to make split-second changes from note to note and to move with the multiple variations in power. A great part of the drama is in the body language—sounds come from the belly of the body, subtle displays of strength are shown in head and arm movements. I'm no expert in the field, but Ban-sensei was good.

Suddenly, I am carried away. I see my father with our old Victrola carefully changing the needle and setting the *shigin* record (he'd bought in LA) on the tiny spindle. He winds the hand crank and turns on the Victrola. He sits on a kitchen chair, leans back, and closes his eyes. He is brown from the sun, his hands are rough from fieldwork, but he is still a young man. Tears choke my throat. And then, just as suddenly, it is over.

Amidst the scattered applause, Ban-sensei shuffled back to his place against the wall. I turned to my daughter Joy and said, "Isn't he wonderful?"

"He's a little clumsy," Joy said.

"He's wearing clogs; he's not use to them." Even as I said this, a thought flashed through: in the years of grueling study, the easiest lesson should have been the first: to walk like a samurai. Swagger. Lucas does it all the time.

I wanted to go to Ban-sensei and tell him how great he was, but why would he care what a stooped old woman says? If I were young and pretty, maybe. No, why should that make a difference? If I didn't do this thing, I'd think about it all afternoon. That's me: obsessive. I should just go up there and do it. Not for him; for myself.

So I did. I said to Ban-sensei, "You were wonderful." Original, huh?

He looked at the floor and smiled. "Thank you," he said.

"You must have studied for many years," I said.

Still looking down, he said, "Yes, thank you."

Alyctra had finished her conference and joined us at the table. "Alyctra," I said, "don't you think he's handsome?" She knew exactly whom I meant.

"Yeah," she said. "He's in my history class."

"What? He's only sixteen?"

"Yeah," she said.

Only sixteen. "And they call him sensei?" I asked.

"He teaches Japanese here."

"Did he spend a lot of time in Japan? That's where he trained, right?"

"I suppose."

"Why didn't you say 'hello' to him?" I asked.

"I didn't say I knew him. We're just in the same class." And then, "He's very quiet. Not very sociable. Keeps to himself."

"He's *hapa*, right?" I asked.

"Oh no, Grammy," Alyctra said. "That lady standing next to him is his mother, and she's from Japan and his last name is Japanese, so he's not *hapa*." Alyctra knew a lot about him for not "knowing" him.

"And his hair is black-black," Joy said.

His hair is black, but the texture isn't Japanese. But I didn't say that. "Is he lame?" I asked.

"Well, first he came to class with his foot in a cast, then he walked on crutches for a while. Then he got some kind of surgery and he walked with a walker for another... while, and now he's walking without help. He kind of scrunches down. He loses two inches that way. Two inches!" That seemed to make her angry. She brought her palm out like an open book and put her face very close to it. "He studies like this," she said. She'd been watching him.

I thought of Ban-sensei as a little boy in Japan. He would stand out. They would know he's *hapa*. I read in the papers that bullying is persistent and brutal in elementary school there, and child victims have been known to commit suicide. I wondered if Ban-sensei was one of the survivors.

He had changed into a T-shirt and baggy pants and had returned to the wall. He did indeed look like a sixteen-year-old kid. Amazing what clothes can do. In a *hakama* he was a young man, tall and handsome, confident at the microphone, a first-class performer.

"Would you do something for me, Alyctra?" I asked.

"Sure," she said and then hesitated. "What?" she asked.

"The next time you see Ban-sensei, would you say hello to him?"

"For you?" she asked.

Yeah, girl, for you too. Feel the fullness of compassion, open the door, watch your horizon expand. But I didn't say that. I only said, "For you too."

A Nisei Writer in America

When I was a little girl, my father bought a set of *The Book of Knowledge,* which was twenty fat books very much like the encyclopedia. I poured over pictures of great men and mysterious drawings of fossil bones that lay buried under our very feet, and classic paintings and illustrations of famous stories and poems.

I couldn't read English, but I was eager to go to school and find the key that would open up the secrets of these books. When I did learn to read, I thought of writers as unapproachably brilliant, and if I entertained thoughts of one day writing, it was buried way down deep. I thought it took years of study to be a writer, and I was too lazy for that.

It was much later that I found almost anyone can write. What is important is to have a love of words and a story you want to tell, a statement you want to make, and an intense and passionate need to tell it. And to write it in a way that readers can say, "Ah, I know that feeling well."

There are many ways of writing. I chose the easiest way, which is to explore the life or conditions or problems of an ordinary person, like myself, in language that's easily understood, about emotions common to everyone—about things we all know and fight for or against: love, hate, jealousy, anger, sorrow, greed, joy.

I write about what I know, which is the life of the Nisei. I write short stories and plays about our concerns, our heritage, and our children. All my stories arise from these problems and situations I share with most

This essay was first delivered as a lecture for the University of Tokyo in October 2001.

Nisei. I set my stories in the time and places I have known. I move on as eras end, laws, and attitudes change, and as I grow and learn. I try to keep true to my characters.

We as human beings are not born from seeds drifting on a wind. Like all animals we have genes, we have ancestors, but we also have historical and cultural backgrounds that make us think and feel the way we do, that decide the roads we take. These decisions are sometimes unconscious, sometimes very deliberate.

True life follows the pattern of cause and effect. True stories are carried over a span of years and generations, and cause and effect are often hard to trace and are lost in the dust of myths. And who cares? We're born to people through no choice of our own; we often carry their neuroses; we do the best we can under the circumstances and do not always question the past that is responsible for the present and the future.

Fictional lives also are woven from cause and effect. Whole stories and plays can be drawn from just five minutes of a situation or can stretch over generations, but cause and effect must be established quickly and clearly. That's what draws our readers into our world and helps them to understand the dilemmas, the triumphs, the heartbreak, and the joy.

Characters do not hang in a void. They are set in a time, they are from a specific social system, an economic class. They wear furs or rags. They may drink from champagne flutes, jelly glasses, chipped tea cups, plastic designer bottles. These details tell the reader who the people are and give us a clue to the focus of their struggles.

And I believe that fictional life, like real life, is governed by the politics of the time, is moved and changed by national and international economics and cultural and personal pressures.

My stories begin with my parents. My father immigrated to America when he was eighteen, in 1905. Most of the men and boys who left Japan at that time were from large farm families, but my father was the first-born son of a *kamaboko-ya* (a fishcake maker) in Shimizu. He was a quiet man and did not speak much of his life in Japan, or, for that matter, his life in America as a young man.

I know this much: he did not *have* to go to America. As the first-born son, he stood to inherit his father's *kamaboko-ya,* but he was young and adventurous. It occurred to me much later that maybe he came to

America to avoid being drafted into the Japanese army. But he wouldn't admit that even in his dreams.

I suppose he had heard of the riches in America and had hoped to pick his share of the gold off the streets. That was the famous story: there was gold on the streets of America. He worked in a dairy, a laundry, and wherever he could earn a few dollars, and he sent money and gifts home to his family. In 1919, when he was thirty-two, he returned to Japan in modest prosperity to find a bride. He planned to go back to America with his wife and to start a farm, hoping to buy a patch of land—a long-range plan. A *baishakunin* (marriage broker) arranged a meeting with my mother's family, and the marriage was set.

After the wedding, the newlyweds set sail for America. My mother promised her sisters she would return in great wealth and pull the family up from an unfortunate loss of face and fortune in their small Shizuoka village.

My father took my mother to a desert farmland north of the Mexican border called Imperial Valley, a hot dry area that was dependent on water diverted from the Colorado River for agricultural and living purposes. There was already a community of Japanese settled there. Because of racism, Asian farmers did not always have access to fertile or desirable locations. With hard work and determination, they made the valley livable and sometimes even profitable, but that was rare.

My mother lived more than half her life there, bringing up four children almost by herself, taking on both hardship and opportunity with a certain stubborn will. She came from a family of strong women, and she would not allow herself to be a victim.

The Nisei grew up during this period—the 1920s and 1930s. The country was deep in depression, but as children we were largely unaware of the desperate times. Everyone was in the same boat. The Issei worked hard, and we did our best to help them; we worked in the fields and mom-and-pop stores from a very early age.

I was born in the year of the Asian Exclusion Act. This new law cut off all Asian immigration to the United States. Up to that time, Japanese men who entered America legally were able to send for brides through picture-bride agencies. The Asian Exclusion Act put an end to that.

There were many men in our community who were caught in the

Asian Exclusion net. These men could not send for brides, could not marry outside the race (again by law), and consequently could not have families. Many single men moved with the crops throughout California, transient laborers working with the seasons, growing old and bent squatting in strawberry patches and harvesting the crops of other people's fields, their dreams of returning to Japan fading in the sun-bleached earth they tilled and the fruits they gathered.

In the years of my family's wanderings, we moved to Oceanside, California, a few hundred miles west of the valley, not far from the Pacific Ocean. The weather was milder, cooler, but our family was totally displaced. We had a disastrous year with a lettuce crop, so we had to move to Oceanside to find work. There were other Japanese families that also left. It was the summer of the Imperial Valley earthquake, and, with many buildings in town damaged and needing repairs, there was a small exodus from the valley.

Oceanside is where I met Hisaye Yamamoto, now an internationally known writer, who is three years older than me and at that time had already been writing stories for the *Kashu Mainichi,* a Japanese-English newspaper published in Los Angeles. Until I found her stories, all the stories I had read were by and about white Americans. This was the first time I consciously realized that we, as a people, didn't have to live in the shadow of white Americans. In spite of the Depression and poverty, in spite of our small number, we had a rich and varied life too. I was fifteen.

The Oceanside Japanese lived mostly in an area called Kumamoto Mura (Kumamoto Village). I cannot say Hisaye Yamamoto was my mentor because she neither encouraged nor discouraged me. But by example she taught me that anything was possible if you kept the faith and prepared yourself for your dreams.

We were in Oceanside in 1941 when war broke out between the United States and Japan. I had a semester more of high school to complete.

Then under Executive Order 9066, signed by President Roosevelt, we Japanese and Japanese Americans on the West Coast were all put into concentration camps—herded like cattle—men, women, and children, young and old, and some very sick people. Armed soldiers guarded us all the way and continued to guard us in camp.

The war that hurt us most, Issei and Nisei alike, is that war with

Japan. It tore us apart, sometimes pitting brother against brother, friend against friend, and sometimes father against son.

It killed many hundreds of Nisei soldiers and maimed many more. These men volunteered for a segregated battalion even though their families remained incarcerated in concentration camps. They fought bravely in Europe and the Pacific and made a name for all of us.

But this war also set aside a group of men who stood up for principle and refused to fight in the American army as long as our families were incarcerated. They were called the Heart Mountain Resisters. Hardly more than boys, they were tried and sent to prison. For many years they were ostracized and led shadowed and shamed lives.

This is the war that divided us, scattered us, united us, separated us, broke our hearts. It made us grow up quickly and sometimes brought about a deeper understanding of ourselves and respect and tolerance for other opinions and beliefs.

But we Nisei are resilient. To this day, we have camp reunions, rejoicing in meeting old friends and talking about those years in camp. East West Players, our Asian American theater in Los Angeles, has produced several plays capturing the Nisei spirit in song and dance, capturing our tendency to joke about the most dire situations and to make the best of it—the *shikata ga nai* attitude that we learned from our parents. I wrote a play called *12-1-A*, which was my address in camp. My family was sent to Poston, Arizona, which interned more than 15,000 Japanese and Japanese Americans during the war. East West Players produced *12-1-A* in 1982.

I met Hiromi Ozaki when she came to see *12-1-A* at East West Players. She asked me then for permission to translate the play into Japanese, and, some years later, she produced it in Tokyo for a limited run. She did a tremendous job translating and finding a producer and theater for the play.

I met Hisaye Yamamoto again in camp. We worked on the camp paper, the *Poston Chronicle*—I was a staff artist, and she was a reporter. We became good friends there. From Hisaye I learned about books and writers, and, more important, I learned about honesty and empathy.

It's been almost sixty years. Since then Hisaye and I have laughed together, cried together, and have had our quarrels, but to this day we are close friends. She has listened patiently for hours on the phone while I read her the stories I had written.

I was born when girls were only expected to grow up and marry and have children. I had dreamed of being a painter, but I fully expected to do this while fulfilling my wifely and motherly duties.

I never expected to be a writer. After I married and my daughter Joy started school, I began to write more seriously. Still it was only sporadically: once a year I wrote a short story for the *Rafu Shimpo* holiday edition. The editor had also worked on the *Poston Chronicle* in camp, and he generously accepted my stories with the provision that I draw illustrations for the holiday edition.

I was already in my mid-thirties. "And the Soul Shall Dance" is the first story I truly worked on and wrote to the finish. When people ask me how long it took to write this eight-page short story, I answer, "Thirty-six years."

I thought it was a good story, so I sent it out to mainstream magazines, but it was always rejected. After a while I didn't care any more whether white America liked my stories. I decided to continue writing about the Japanese in America as honestly and deeply as I could.

In the meantime, ethnic diversity became more acceptable in America, and young Asian American educators established Asian American studies centers at various colleges and universities. About this time, Hisaye told me that four young professors, Jeffrey Chan, Frank Chin, Lawson Inada, and Shawn Wong, were putting together an anthology of Asian American writers to use in their classes. Hisaye suggested I send them something.

They accepted "And the Soul Shall Dance" for their book *Aiiieeeee! An Anthology of Asian American Writers*. Mako, then director of East West Players, read my story and asked me to adapt it into a play for his theater.

I was really torn. I had never written a play, hardly ever went to them, didn't enjoy reading them, and yet I didn't want anyone else tampering with my story. I didn't know what to do.

At that time, my twenty-five-year marriage had fallen apart, my daughter was in college, and I had no more duties as wife and mother. After examining my life, I realized I had never given myself totally to anything I had undertaken.

I had decided to study painting and put all my effort into it. And now Mako asked me to write a play. When he noticed my hesitancy, he said, "Well, think about it."

Not a week later, I broke my leg falling from a chair eighteen inches high. I was in the hospital for days and afterwards had to lie in bed for a month with my leg in a cast. I couldn't go to my art classes. It was like fate making my decision for me.

There weren't many Asian American playwrights at that time. There were Frank Chin and Momoko Iko. Later I heard of Ed Sakamoto, Jon Shirota, and Bill Shinkai. There were others, but I was not in touch with the theater world.

I was very unsure of myself. At one point I told Mako that I couldn't do it. I was not a playwright. I could not write like Chin or Iko.

Mako said he didn't care how I wrote the play; he didn't care if it was a hit or a flop. All he asked from me was a promise to keep the mood of the story in the play. I shall never forget that. That was the beginning of my playwriting life.

I have heard Mako say that first production of *And the Soul Shall Dance* at East West Players was one of the memorable experiences of his long directorial, producing, and acting career. I could not have written it without his help and vote of confidence. He has always kept the play close to his heart, and in 2001 he and producer Yoichi Aoki (Aerial U.S., Inc.) translated the script into Japanese and presented it along with the Teoriza Theater in Tokyo with Hiromi Ozaki (of *12-1-A*) in the lead.

I shall never forget that first time I saw it in Tokyo. This was the true language of the play. I did the best I could in English but did not quite capture the essence of the Issei. These were the Japanese who left their beloved Japan to pick the gold off the streets of America, found vastly less, and swallowed their disappointment in samurai spirit with a laugh, a joke, a girding of the loins. And in the ashes of their dreams, they found their true strength.

Although this story is three or four generations removed from most Japanese audiences, I hope they will see how much love and longing the Issei had for the country of their birth—the unrequited love, the longing never answered. This you will know only when you leave the beloved country of your birth. In your heart there will always be a small ache reminding you that a place waits for your return. The dancers pause. The singers call. The fireflies await.

My Mother's Cooking

My father farmed in the arid Southern California desert just north of the Mexican border. My mother often helped him in the fields. She got up in the morning, fixed our breakfast of hot rice, miso soup, and preserved cabbage, and sent us off to school with our brown-bag lunches: jam sandwiches, a cookie, and an apple.

In the late afternoon she came in from the fields and cooked supper on a three-burner kerosene stove. She did not make a ceremony of cooking, using her hands often: a handful of this, a dollop of that, a dribble or pinch of the other. For treats she made huge pancakes the size of the skillet and tore them into manageable pieces for us. Sometimes she baked cookies or made forlorn little orange pies in our oven, a metal box set over a burner. An orange pie is like a lemon pie only made with oranges.

I think how tired she must have been at the end of the day, but I suppose our happy faces were among her few joys, and, with the pancakes and orange pies, she tried to be as American as we were growing to be. I didn't care much for the rather doughy skillet cakes, but I tried to put on a good face because I knew instinctively that my mother depended on it. My brother was a voracious eater, and he could be counted on to finish everything on my plate. He loved those pancakes. He'd reach for them, shouting happily, "Gimme one of them horse blankets!"

We ate from our vegetable garden and from the farm: tomatoes, cucumbers, summer squash, snow peas, eggplant, Chinese cabbage, carrots, beets, and spinach. Except for a few chickens, we did not keep livestock, so we ate very little meat. Chickens were slaughtered only for special occasions: Thanksgiving, Christmas (though we were not Christians), New Year's.

116

Sometimes the food we ate embarrassed us: soy sauce was bug juice to white Americans and no Japanese kid admitted to eating raw fish. It seemed barbaric. Once our third-grade teacher asked the class to name ways of preparing fish. "Fried!" we called out. "Baked!" "Broiled!" And one trusting Japanese boy proudly offered, "Raw!" The class tittered.

"Raw?" our teacher screamed. "You are mistaken!" We who were Japanese laughed too. We did not stand by the mortified boy.

Except for brief forays into American cooking, my mother stuck with Japanese foods, making adjustments and substitutions for unavailable items. Sometimes a change of one ingredient ruined the whole dish for me, and I would grumble without regard or sympathy for the difficulties of keeping a culture alive in a foreign land. Still, sometimes I'd watch her at her chores and wonder if I would ever have the stamina to be the person she was. It wasn't easy for a woman. It wasn't easy for a man either.

My father had come to America earlier than my mother. He'd spent his bachelor years at a lot of jobs and had acquired a taste for foods alien to the Japanese palate: cheese, ham, beef, head cheese, and the abhorrent pickled pigs' feet that he would have with his *sake*. He taught us to gnaw on and enjoy the little pink piglet toes. On the whole he was a serious man. He tolerated no nonsense at the supper table and restored order by clearing his throat loudly. Our bickering ceased instantly.

Our family left the farm in the summer of 1939 after the great Imperial Valley earthquake and after a disastrous year with a lettuce crop. We have not cleaned lamp chimneys or cooked on kerosene stoves since. Over gas burners and real ovens the food remained largely Japanese, but we began to experience hot dogs and hamburgers, sometimes on buns, more often sitting in a pool of soy or teriyaki sauce along with vegetables in season.

I was a picky eater and did not find much interest in food or in cooking. After World War II, I broke away from the family, married, and found myself ill-prepared for wifely duties. Although my husband preferred Japanese food, I could never match my mother-in-law's devotion and commitment to Japanese cuisine. We ate American style. After a while I learned to cook the way my husband liked, and it was often a pleasure to watch my family at the supper table. Like my mother, I loved to see them happy.

I am single now and a rather solitary person. As I grow I return to the foods of my childhood. They settle in my stomach like old friends, faults forgotten, sins forgiven. They affirm the past and stabilize the future. I revert to my mother's method of cooking. "Improvise! Adjust"; she sends a silent message useful outside the kitchen as well.

Fortunately for me, many sauces are found in the Asian section of the supermarket: teriyaki sauce (good with meat and poultry), black bean sauce (delicious with pork and tofu), plum sauce (a great glaze for chicken), oyster sauce (good with anything). In the recipe I offer, no ingredient or measurement is carved in stone. Take a chance; improvise.

Stir-Fried Whatever

2 tablespoons of sesame or vegetable oil
2 medium broccoli spears in 1½ inch slices
Half a bunch of asparagus, sliced diagonally
8 ounces of sliced white mushrooms
½ cup of sliced onions
½ cup of sliced bell pepper
½ cup of diagonally sliced celery
⅓ cup of oyster sauce
1 teaspoon of cornstarch
⅓ cup of water
(optional: thin strips of chicken, beef, or pork, about ¼ pound)

If meat is used, sauté in hot sesame oil until browned. Add onions, celery, bell pepper. Stir-fry broccoli, asparagus, and mushrooms in the same skillet. Do not overcook. Dissolve cornstarch in water and add to oyster sauce, mixing well. Stir sauce into vegetables and cook quickly until gravy thickens. Serve with (or over) hot rice. This dish should take about fifteen minutes to prepare. Serves about four.

On the days I pick up my granddaughter from school, I prepare dinner for the family. We sit on the front room floor and have supper at the coffee table while watching *Jeopardy*. I love the talking and laughing and, yes, the scolding and whining that go on. These are the bonus years.

Taj Mahal

The play *Taj Mahal* started out as an experiment, an exercise: to try writing from a white man's point of view. The time I chose was the 1930s, the time of America's Great Depression, when many men from the lowest economic rung, jobless and homeless, were riding the rails looking to change their lives. I felt I knew a little about being broke and searching for a change. My narrator was a fifty-year-old white transient who had spent most of his youth in aimless wandering. Now he was old, his best years squandered, and he faced a future of strangling loneliness.

The play was a short monologue delivered to an almost unseen youth. The old man speaks about his past, running away from an abusive alcoholic father and working from one end of the country to the other, east to west and back again, driving cattle to Chicago stockyards, doing odd jobs, always on the move, searching for utopia and freedom and never finding either. He speaks of a love affair that he relives again and again, a story he hopes to sell one day. He tells the tale to the inattentive boy (wrapped up in his own problems), who he sees as the ghost of himself as a young man. He tries to make connection with the youth through his own experiences, particularly that of the one romantic encounter that he remembers as a young man.

The love affair is a seduction by his boss's daughter, who lures him into the main ranch house to see pictures through a stereoscope. Among the landscapes is the Taj Mahal, a monument to love that a shah had built for one of his wives. Lost on the old man is why a prince with access to so many women found only one to capture his heart. Doesn't that prove something right there? But I digress.

The boss comes home; the young man runs out with his clothes under his arm, the stereoscope caught in the folds. The brief paradise he found with the boss's daughter and his swift and awkward exit remain in his mind until he is an old man, though the fear of the angry father and his loaded gun had faded. The stereoscope had been hocked or sold or lost many years ago. Well, what good is a stereoscope without the special pictures anyway? The beautiful Taj Mahal, for instance.

As he tells the story, it occurs to the old man that one can go through life without seeing or experiencing its fullness—like the flat pictures that come to the eye in unimagined depth and delight when seen through a stereoscope. Maybe it's not too late to change the emptiness of one's existence. The disinterested boy rushes off to catch an eastbound freight.

So it goes. It may take the kid a long time before he sees the Taj Mahal in its total splendor. Maybe he'll one day make his way to Agra not knowing why. Well hell, there's even time for the old man to hop a boat and make a pilgrimage to the beautiful Taj Mahal.

I called the sketch "The Stereoscope" and left it with the artistic director of East/West Players, an Asian American theater company in Los Angeles.

East/West Players was the first Asian American theater in the United States. It was established by a group of Asian American actors who were tired of the stereotypic roles they were always hired for, few and far between as they were, and they set about founding their own theater where they could be seen beyond the character of the evil Asian or the exotic lotus blossom. East/West was an equity waiver theater (the actors do not get paid), and as such, the East/West actors endured many years of hardship and hanging together. That meant they kept programs going through thick and thin, with everyone pitching in, working the lights and the sound, building sets, cleaning toilets, mopping floors, making repairs, patching the roof. All this without anyone getting paid.

In summer there were workshops in acting, movement, playwriting, music, and voice. At the end of the session, there was a "finale" of sorts, an evening when the students showed what they had learned. Although "The Stereoscope" was not appropriate for an Asian American theater (both characters were white Americans), one of the actors in the workshop selected it for his final piece that summer. I was invited to the program.

The instructor of the program, Rick Edelstein, a well-known character actor in his day, said "The Stereoscope" should be expanded. He asked me to reveal who the kid was, why he didn't talk, what his problem was. He was depressed, yes. Was he suicidal?

Well, the kid could have been a doorknob or a sweater on a peg. I only needed someone to be there so the audience would know the old man wasn't just talking to himself—a clear-cut nut case. I was delighted that this was the only criticism I got, and I considered my experiment a success. Rick didn't say the sketch wasn't working or was not believable. He only said he wanted more from me.

"Okay," I said and put it in my unfinished play file.

Years have passed since; two other artistic directors followed the original pioneering man. East/West dropped the slash, moved into a larger space, and East West Players became "legitimate." The new theater is much grander with a first-class stage and high-tech gear. It is no longer an equity waiver theater.

In the days of the old ninety-nine-seat theater, actors, writers, and directors grew like family with each new production, and, later as we moved on, we would contact one another when we heard of job opportunities.

Rodney Kageyama, who directed my play *12-1-A* in a very fine production at UCLA's Freud Playhouse in 1992, called me one day and asked if I had an unproduced play that he might direct for a reading. He had access to space at the Japanese American National Museum. East West Players only did readings of plays from their writers' workshop; it was too costly to open the theater for plays from outside sources, I was told. These readings are to help writers hear the dialogue and make changes if necessary.

I write plays about Japanese Americans. My plays are about our immigrant experience, about our incarceration in camps as young adults during World War II *(12-1-A)*. As I grow older, my plays embrace the problems of seniors coping with old age and memories that won't let go.

Well, it happened that I had two unproduced one-act plays. Rodney selected seasoned actors for the reading, and the plays went very well. However, the reading wasn't well attended because it played on the same night as a huge, formal Asian American theater awards dinner. I got favorable comments, but all the heavyweights were at the awards show. I didn't get one bite from an interested producer.

A few years later, Rodney asked if I had other unproduced material. Well, I had this one sketch. "Let me look at it," he said. I gave him "Stereoscope."

Rodney found "The Stereoscope" interesting, but, like Rick Edelstein, he wanted more. "Make it a two-act play," he said. He had actor friends who were between jobs, so he asked me to change the white hobo to a black man and the silent boy to a Japanese kid. Easy for him to say, I thought.

Changing the hobo to a black man meant a major shift in the story. Racism was rampant in the thirties. Black people would experience it whether they worked in the White House (at that time, very unlikely unless as servants), as Pullman porters, or as hobos riding the rails. A black man of the thirties would be well aware of American racism. He would experience it every day of his life. It would be a given. An uneducated black man who worked in the coal mines of Pennsylvania and ran away from his abusive father would speak in a regional dialect. He would not expect favors from the white man. And it would be a long time before he would be seated in a white restaurant or permitted to use a public restroom. Even after the freedom movement twenty years later, there were incidences of lynching and at least one bombing of a black church. The thirties were difficult times for everyone, especially minorities.

I called the hobo Jake, a man who found freedom only among his own people or alone. But Jake's people were an alcoholic father and an abusive mother. He had no friends. He chose to be alone. He left his family at fifteen with the clothes on his back, the shoes on his feet, and his lunch pail. I chose the dialect used by the Pennsylvania blacks in August Wilson's plays.

I didn't see much chance of writing a play about a black man and getting it produced in either an Asian or a black theater. Among the blacks, I would be regarded as an interloper. My focus would have to be on the Japanese boy if I hoped for a production.

There were many transient laborers in the thirties, but there would not be young Japanese hobos. Japanese tend to keep their families together no matter how tough the going. They stayed together as they scratched a meager living off the land or lived on the nickels and dimes of immigrant trade. Japanese families helped one another through bad times. Orphaned children were often adopted by relatives, neighbors, or friends. Boys were especially important in the Asian American economy. They worked in the farms; they drove trucks; they spoke English and read contracts. There would not be many Japanese American runaways.

My Japanese boy would have come from Japan. A young Japanese immigrant who considers suicide in America had to be in deep trouble. He would have left Japan because of unbearable conditions there. The Asian Exclusion Act, passed in 1924, would not allow him to enter America legally, so he would be an illegal immigrant. Because of the antimiscegenation law, he would not have a romantic life. He would, perhaps, be faithful to the memory of his mother or his sister. He would be hounded by the authorities and haunted by promises he had not kept.

Some years before I wrote "Stereoscope," I read an oral history of a small village in Japan called Nagaya. The editor had put together a book of the residents' experience in the mid-thirties. The community as it was then was disappearing, and the stories were fading from memory. The editor had lived in Nagaya as a boy, and he remembered the villagers and the hardship they had endured. He wanted a record of those times, so he compiled a book of interviews that he called *Silk and Straw*.

There were years of famine; many women died giving birth because of malnutrition. The peasants wore the same rags in summer and winter, patched and repatched, until they literally fell off their backs. They were always hungry. Children worked in rice paddies or as carters along with adults. Carters were people who pulled carts of merchandise from the seaport to warehouses to outlying villages and retail stores. Horses were not practical, first because almost no one had the money to buy one, and further, a horse had to be fed and washed and kept warm in winter and cool in summer. They were more trouble than people.

This is where my boy would come from, Nagaya. I called him Jun because it sounds like "John." He lost his mother at five (she bled to death while giving birth), and his sister, Iku, had taken care of him until he turned nine, when he went to work with his father as a carter. At seventeen, he conspired to leave his dear sister and walk to Yokohama to stow away on a ship to America, where he would jump ship in San Francisco. That was his plan. He was tired of being hungry, tired of wearing rags, and angry at his father for being so powerless. He would go to America and work and send money so Iku would have a grand dowry and a chance to marry a wealthy man. He did not want her to marry another poor carter and continue this legacy of sickness and poverty. He owed her that. She had grown so thin.

Iku pleaded with him to stay. Without him she would die, she cried. No, he reasoned. If he stayed, they would both die—she, like their mother, slowly bleeding to death and he, broken with hopelessness. But if he were to find work in America, he could send her money. Or better still, he would come back rich and build a house and start a business. They would be respected members of the community. They would never starve again. Iku would have a proper dowry. He would come back to Japan to marry too, and they would be happy forever, maybe living together in one big, wonderful house with horses in the stable.

He leaves with the memory of Iku pleading and weeping and he, soothing, scolding, and promising, promising. He sneaks out without saying good-bye to his father.

In America, Jun keeps one step ahead of the immigration authorities, moving from place to place, job to job. He works in restaurants, eating well and wearing good clothes—it's not smart to look like an immigrant. He is haunted by the image of his sweet, sacrificing sister, but the grand plan is to save money and later open a restaurant of his own, grow rich, and return to Japan in glory. Unknowingly, he is slowly being seduced by American materialism.

Betrayed by a fellow worker, Jun is again on the run with his blanket roll and his money. He hopes to go south to San Diego, where a community of Japanese reside. By the side of the road, he writes a letter to Iku, assuring her it will not be long now; he can already see her happy face; didn't he tell her to have faith? Like all his other letters to her, this one also does not get mailed.

He stops at a roadside eatery to restore his energy. He gets involved with a con-artist who could use help in selling snake oil from the back of his truck. No, Jun is determined to continue to San Diego, and, as the man says good-bye and passes his friendly hand over Jun's shoulder and lightly down, he lifts Jun's wallet and leaves.

The cafe owner is disgusted with the idiot who would let this happen and directs Jun to the freight yard, the hobo jungle, a good place for losers like Jun.

Jun is disgusted too. Angry at the thief, at fate, at himself, so pitifully selfish he did not send money to his sister, not even five dollars that would have put fish on her table and also replaced her worn straw sandals. He isn't worthy of her, not worthy of his promise as a man, not worthy of life. He veers close to the railroad tracks. There is hardly a soul around. Only one black man.

And so fate and the economies of two nations conspired for the meeting of these two men at the lowest points of their lives. At a windswept freight yard, one considers suicide; the other thinks he has found a friend in this lonely, desperate young man.

Jun had never seen blacks in Nagaya, and those he's seen in San Francisco were locked in the lowest jobs: dishwashers, street sweepers, janitors. With his island mentality, he trusts no one—black and white alike, scheming yellows too, but especially white men with slick talk. He just wants to wallow alone in his depression.

With persistence, Jake begins to open a dialogue, talking about his family, his wanderings, but he mainly tries to change the boy's state of mind. Jun reluctantly reveals the promises he made to his sister Iku.

No problem there. Why, they could be partners, Jake says; together they would make their way south, Jake would sell his story to Hollywood, and he'd help raise money for Iku too. Jake turns alive with plans. This is the end of his solitary existence, never again to be lonely and dying without anyone, anyone caring. Oh, the adventures that await! They could do it all, together.

But Jun must fulfill the promise to Iku on his own, without help. Especially from a black man. In spite of his racist attitudes, Jun allows Jake to bring hope into his life. He relaxes, he sleeps, he finds new momentum, and now he must go.

Jake tries to persuade Jun to stay with him, to go south to Hollywood to live the free life. In desperation, he reveals the secret story he plans to sell, the story of his love affair with Mary Ann, the red-haired daughter of his despicable white boss. She had lured him into the main house with a picture of the Taj Mahal mounted on the stereoscope. Ever see a picture through a stereoscope? Full, deep, so real, the leaves on the trees seem to tremble.

No one would believe that story, Jun laughs. A black man with a white woman? Forget the story, forget the girl, forget the Taj. It's just a picture, just a dream.

It's not just a picture. Not just a dream. It's a monument to love, that Taj. But one needs a special lens to see it right. The lens is the important thing. Just like the two of them here. One day Jun will find that lens and see in Jake the fullness of the man he really is. And they will live the wholeness of life as it was meant to be.

Well, yes, the Taj is a dream. It's Jun's dream of returning to Japan rich. It's Jake's dream of selling his story. And maybe one day they will both find their Taj. But not together. And not in the thirties.

And that's the end of that.

I tried to tell the story of an almost forgotten day in a man's past that is more emotional than he remembered. Now I had to find a way to make it pertinent to now, today, to catch a sense of having lost something of intangible value that cannot be retrieved. Never relived. The time is gone. And though the sun rises and sets daily on the same dusty piece of Fresno, the place is gone, the hobo jungle is gone. The newspapers swirling in the wind disintegrated long ago. The little sandwich shop has been demolished. The people are gone. Only the story remains in one man's head.

After several false starts, I decided to open the play in the present. Jun is now an octogenarian. He has been found in Los Angeles' Little Tokyo wandering aimlessly, walking heedlessly into the traffic. He does not identify himself or reveal his address, so he is put under observation in the county hospital.

At the hospital, a black orderly and a thin Asian American nurse try to get information from him: what is his name, address; who are his people, his friends? How long has he been in the United States? Where are his papers? Where are his people?

Although Jun withholds the pertinent stuff, he most reluctantly tells them his best friend Yamada died the week before. They'd been together since "camp" days when they worked in the mess halls in one of America's concentration camps during the war with Japan. They had spent over half a century together, leaving camp together, working, eating, boozing together, and gambling in those casinos. Now Yamada is dead, and from the other side, in the light at the end of the tunnel, he gives Jun no peace, every night beckoning. "Come...come...."

Total bunk? All Jun really needs is a good night's sleep. The black orderly promises to look into a release in the morning. Everyone's entitled to a period of grief, a little craziness. Perfectly normal. This is no place for a sane man; it's a loony bin, for crying out loud. A little sedative might help.

Could it be the skinny nurse resembled Iku? Did the black orderly bring to mind a forgotten friend from so long ago? Whatever, they are all there in Jun's drug-induced sleep, the thief who stole his wallet, the black hobo, his pungent unwashed smell fusing with the October dust.

His friend Yamada is there. But he's appearing nightly, always beckoning, admonishing Jun not to ask for too much, not to think too deeply, it's all simply a dream. Living or dying. All the same. Like an old vaudeville act. Don't worry, it'll all come back.

Yamada disappears, and other dead ones take over and replay that day on the road and in the freight yard. Iku, long buried in a Nagaya cemetery, young and sweet again, weeping, "Don't go, don't go. I will die. You will forget me," haunting, her tears falling, falling; Iku who looked after his every need like a true mother, and he, the faithless brother, letting the white man rob him and take all he had, and Jake, talking, talking, talking, and that callow Jun, well, that Jun is dead, too. Ah...he should have sent her half...all...all the money, if he were going to be robbed anyway. What a fool he was.

"Don't die!" Jun calls out. "I'll send the money. I have lots of money!" Yes, the redress for those four years of incarceration in that camp. So long ago.

He wakes. In the dim light he sees that he is alone in a hospital room. A good time to leave. He tries the door. Locked. Well, tomorrow. The orderly said tomorrow he will be released.

Tomorrow he will go to the bank and draw out the money. He will buy tickets to India. He will pay for everything. Everything. Jake, do you hear?

Too late. Everyone's gone. Everyone. Well, of course, nobody lives forever. He will go to India for all of them. He will see the beautiful Taj for all of them. That's the dream, is it not?

Production Notes for
Yamauchi / ROSEBUD AND OTHER STORIES

Cover design by Julie Matsuo-Chun

Interior design and composition by Wanda China in
    Minion Pro with display type in Clearface Antique

Printing and binding by Sheridan Books, Inc.

Printed on 60 lb. House Opaque, 500 ppi